'Have you asked.

His teasing smile sent her heart racing. 'No,' Vicky replied automatically as she forced herself to stop focusing on her reaction to him.

'Then why are you stuck in the corner? I thought this gathering was in your family's honour.'

'It is.' She shrugged.

'Then, as the only member of your family here, wouldn't that make you the guest of honour?'

'Perhaps. Most people here have found themselves in a similar situation—the sale of their family land. So I'd say it's more a gathering of kindred spirits.'

'That land means a lot to you, doesn't it?'

'It did. It doesn't really matter now. What's done is done. I guess I should try and look on the bright side.'

Lucy Clark began writing romance in her early teens and immediately knew she'd found her 'calling' in life. After working as a secretary in a busy teaching hospital, she turned her hand to writing medical romance. She currently lives in Adelaide, Australia, and has the desire to travel the world with her husband. Lucy largely credits her writing success to the support of her husband, family and friends.

Recent titles by the same author:

POTENTIAL DADDY

POTENTIAL HUSBAND

BY
LUCY CLARK

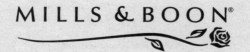

MILLS & BOON®

To Ruth—wonderful mother-in-law, wonderful friend.
Thank you for your support. Ruth 1:16

DID YOU PURCHASE THIS BOOK WITHOUT A COVER?

If you did, you should be aware it is **stolen property** as it was reported *unsold and destroyed* by a retailer. Neither the author nor the publisher has received any payment for this book.

All the characters in this book have no existence outside the imagination of the author, and have no relation whatsoever to anyone bearing the same name or names. They are not even distantly inspired by any individual known or unknown to the author, and all the incidents are pure invention.

All Rights Reserved including the right of reproduction in whole or in part in any form. This edition is published by arrangement with Harlequin Enterprises II B.V. The text of this publication or any part thereof may not be reproduced or transmitted in any form or by any means, electronic or mechanical, including photocopying, recording, storage in an information retrieval system, or otherwise, without the written permission of the publisher.

This book is sold subject to the condition that it shall not, by way of trade or otherwise, be lent, resold, hired out or otherwise circulated without the prior consent of the publisher in any form of binding or cover other than that in which it is published and without a similar condition including this condition being imposed on the subsequent purchaser.

MILLS & BOON and MILLS & BOON with the Rose Device are registered trademarks of the publisher.

First published in Great Britain 2000
Harlequin Mills & Boon Limited,
Eton House, 18-24 Paradise Road, Richmond, Surrey TW9 1SR

© Lucy Clark 2000

ISBN 0 263 82228 1

Set in Times Roman 10½ on 11½ pt.
03-0004-54358

Printed and bound in Spain
by Litografía Rosés, S.A., Barcelona

CHAPTER ONE

'WHAT the…?'

Vicky peered through the dirty windscreen and slowed her car. Andrew Anderson, with a red and worried face, dressed in dark T-shirt and track pants, was frantically waving his arms around. She pulled to the side of the road and parked behind a shiny blue Jaguar, and the twelve-year-old boy rushed to the window.

'Doc,' he puffed. 'Boy, am I glad to see you. Neil's been bitten by a snake and we need help. You've got to call the ambulance. I stopped a man,' he said, pointing to the Jaguar, 'and he's a doctor, but he told me to come back and find someone who lived here so they could call the ambulance.'

Vicky climbed out of the car and glanced briefly at her watch as she collected the black medical bag and portable stretcher from the tailgate of her station wagon. She resigned herself to having less time to shower and change for her afternoon appointment but such was the life of a country doctor.

'I see,' she replied, thankful she was wearing jeans, as they gingerly climbed over the waist-high, barbed-wire fence. Andrew collected the bike he'd left lying on his parents' property and pushed it as they ran carefully over the uneven ground. All this land belonged to his family but this area was one of the furthest boundaries from the homestead.

'The ambulance is already out on another call but should be back at the hospital soon.' She looked at the boy's anxious face. 'Neil will be OK. Why don't you tell me what happened? Did you see the snake?'

'Yep. It was huge and brown,' he replied a little breath-

5

lessly. There was eagerness in his tone and she knew he wanted to help his friend in any way he could. 'We went riding after lunch. Neil wanted to see where the road was so we came down through the paddocks into the bush. We stopped and lazed on a log. Neil…' Andrew shuddered '…put his hand into the log. That's when the snake bit him. We didn't know what'd happened and when we moved away the snake slithered out. It was huge!'

'How long ago did it happen?'

''Bout ten minutes. I figured the road was closer and I could flag down a car faster than riding home. The man, the other doc, stopped straight away. Once I'd showed him where Neil was he told me to go back to the road.'

'Did you see any puncture marks on Neil's hand?'

'Y-yes.' He shuddered again. 'He'll be OK, won't he, Doc? I mean, he has to be. He's me best mate.'

'I'm sure he'll be fine once we get him to hospital.'

'He's over there.' Andrew pointed to a small clearing in the bush where a boy was lying on the ground, a man crouched beside him.

'Hello,' Vicky said to Neil, who gave her a watery smile as she placed her medical bag and stretcher on the ground. She had expected the stranger to look up and acknowledge her, but instead he kept his attention focused on applying a bandage to Neil's arm.

'Have you called for an ambulance?' he barked.

Vicky was momentarily stunned by his dictatorial tone and stammered, 'N-not yet.'

'Why on earth not?' He raised his head and from behind his sunglasses she felt him appraise her figure. She blinked, knowing confusion was portrayed in her dark brown eyes.

'I…I wanted a quick look at the wound first.'

'Are you a nurse?' he asked with a hint of contempt.

'No,' she replied.

She was about to tell him exactly what her profession

was when he said sharply, 'Then stop dallying, girl, and arrange for an ambulance. I presume you know where the closest phone is?'

Grinding her teeth together in an attempt to suppress her anger, Vicky snapped the mobile phone off the waistband of her jeans.

'I presume that's an analogue phone—my digital's out of range,' the stranger said.

Vicky ignored his comment and waited for her call to be answered. 'Nicole,' she said a moment later, 'is the ambulance back yet?' Vicky paused. 'OK. Can you ask Mac to come as soon as possible to the south-eastern boundary of the Anderson farm, just off the town road? Neil Simpson has been bitten by a brown snake so I'll need some antivenene.'

She waited for the director of nursing's brief reply, before hanging up.

'How long will it take to get here?'

'Hopefully no more than twenty minutes,' she replied in a clipped tone.

'Thank you.' The two words were said without sincerity. He went on, 'Now find me a stick I can use as a splint.'

Taking a deep breath, Vicky looked down at Neil and smiled. 'That sounds like a good idea. Andrew and I will find the best stick in the entire bush to splint your arm with.'

Her words made Neil return her smile and she motioned for Andrew to follow her. They walked a short distance away, their eyes glued to the ground in search of a stick that was long and smooth enough.

'Why is that man being so mean to you?' Andrew asked. 'You're the doc. Why don't you do the bandaging?'

As Vicky had suspected, both boys were obviously picking up on the tension between herself and the stranger.

'He's already taking very good care of Neil and we need to help him,' she replied, not wanting to belittle the man in the boy's eyes. 'Mac will be here soon with some antivenene and then we can get Neil off to the hospital where he can receive first-class treatment.'

'How about this one?' Andrew asked, and picked up a stick.

'That looks perfect,' Vicky said. 'Nice and smooth and about the right length. Good going, Andrew.' She patted him on the shoulder and they headed back to the patient.

'I found it,' Andrew said with pride as he handed the stick over. 'Doc Hansen said it was perfect.'

At the boy's words, the stranger tilted his head up to look at her. The dark glasses were still in place and Vicky was irked that he didn't have the decency to remove them. This way she was at a disadvantage and couldn't effectively level him with one of her glaring looks.

'Vet, dentist or medical doctor?' he asked.

He would just love it to be one of the first two, she thought and said with defiance, 'The latter.'

'Well, don't just stand there—assist me with this bandage,' he barked again, making her feel quite silly.

Giving her teeth another grind in frustration, Vicky knelt and held the stick firmly in place as he pulled another crêpe bandage from his own bag, before binding Neil's arm to the splint.

'Mum's gonna do her nut when she finds out, isn't she, Doc?' Neil asked, his voice slightly wavering, anticipating what was to come.

'Would she have been contacted?' the stranger demanded.

'Yes,' Vicky said. 'Our director of nursing will ensure the message is passed on to both of the boys' parents.'

As Vicky continued to hold the stick she became aware of the stranger's closeness. She not only noticed the slight crooked curve in his nose, indicating a break many years ago, but could breathe in the scent of his cologne, which teased her senses.

His hair was short, jet black and lusciously thick. Vicky's fingers instantly itched to touch it but she controlled the urge. His jaw line was strong and angular, confirming the arrogance she had already seen displayed. But his lips... They were slightly parted as he dealt with their small patient and all Vicky could wonder at was how soft they would feel pressed against her own.

She felt her heart rate increase as various images entered her head of the dark stranger's lips pressed passionately to her own in an electrifying embrace. Vicky briefly closed her eyes and sighed before a rustling sound behind her brought her back to the present with a thud.

Glancing over her shoulder, she noticed that Andrew had stepped on pile of twigs and leaves. Silently she thanked him for breaking the spell the stranger's presence had evoked deep within her. What had come over her? She usually displayed a cool, calm and controlled attitude towards the opposite sex.

Good-looking he might be, but as far as manners went he'd definitely missed his share. *Obviously* a city doctor!

Vicky assisted as the bandaging progressed. She schooled her thoughts to her agenda for the rest of the day...

His fingers brushed her arm with an electrifying heat, causing her flesh to develop goose-bumps. The contact startled her and she jerked her head up to look at him, but his concentration was fixed.

The heart she had just managed to control was now beating erratically once more. One simple touch from his hand had evoked an emotion so foreign Vicky might have mistaken it for a heart attack.

When he reached the top end of the stick she was thankful he no longer needed her assistance and relinquished her hold.

Taking a deep breath and grasping her sanity once more, she called to Andrew. 'Would you mind helping me set the stretcher up? We can carry Neil to the road so that when Mac arrives with the ambulance he doesn't have to find us.'

'Sure thing,' he replied, and followed Vicky's instructions. The stretcher was easy enough for one person to assemble but she thought it better to give Andrew something to do, as well as help her occupy her thoughts more professionally.

Once that was done, she turned and smiled down at Neil. 'Not long to go now,' she said soothingly and knelt beside him once more, doing her best to ignore the city doctor. Neil needed to remain as calm as possible to stop the further spread of venom around his body. She brushed a lock of hair from his eyes.

'You're being very brave,' she assured him.

'What about the poison?' he asked, biting his lower lip.

'Mac will bring the antivenene we need to fix you up.'

'Why don't you have any in your bag?' he asked, curiosity getting the better of him.

'I wish I *could* carry it around with me but things like antivenene for snake and spider bites need to be stored in special places, like a fridge, and kept at a constant temperature.'

'I presume your hospital is up to date on all its antivenene stocks?' the man asked.

'Most certainly, Doctor,' Vicky replied, pleased to hear her voice sound as emotionless as his. 'Considering we have more call for them in rural settings, it would be foolish not to.'

Vicky turned her attention back to Neil, watching closely for any signs and symptoms such as drowsiness or nausea. So far he hadn't complained of a headache or any other pain, which was a very good sign.

'As he's one of your patients, Dr Hansen, why don't you perform your observations, then we can transfer him to the stretcher?' the doctor prompted, making Vicky feel even more awkward than before.

She turned and reached for her bag, counting to ten in as calm a manner as she possibly could. 'Now, Neil,' she said as she reached for his wrist, 'I'd like to check your pulse and then I'll shine a light into your eyes—the same way I do when your mum brings you into the clinic for a check-up. OK?'

'Sure. I know that doesn't hurt,' Neil replied bravely.

Her observations proved that Neil was as relaxed as possible, indicating that the blood was pumping around his body at a normal rate and not accelerating the spread of the venom. Hopefully, he shouldn't need more than two or three injections of the antivenene to stop the poison.

Satisfied with his condition, she gave the man a brief nod and moved the stretcher closer. The stranger lifted Neil with ease but Vicky noticed his biceps flex beneath his crisp white shirt. Not only did she find herself attracted to him, she also noticed he had a fantastic body.

She swallowed, unable to look away, and allowed her gaze to take its fill of the rest of him as he stood. He was well over six feet, and from the way his designer-label business suit fitted him she knew it wasn't only his biceps that were in perfect shape.

'What about the bikes?' Andrew asked, and Vicky quickly looked away.

'What?' she asked, frowning at him as his words slowly penetrated the sensual haze. 'Oh, the bikes. Why don't we leave them here and you and your dad can bring the truck down later and collect them? For the moment, I need your muscles to help me carry these medical bags back. Think you can manage?'

'Yup,' he replied, and hoisted a bag in each hand.

'Let's go,' the man said flatly, and waited for Vicky to get into position at the other end of the stretcher. 'The ground is fairly uneven so watch where you step,' he said. 'The last thing we need now is a sprained ankle.'

Of all the nerve! 'You've no need to worry about me, Doctor,' she replied sweetly. 'I'm more than used to the rugged terrain of the country, but accidents do happen so be careful.'

He turned and glared at her, before starting to walk towards the road. Vicky smiled at his back and congratulated herself on her cleverness.

They were nearly at the fence when they heard the wail of the ambulance siren and saw the red and white vehicle coming towards them.

'Here's the cavalry,' he said. They had just finished negotiating the stretcher over the fence when Mac alighted to give them a hand. He opened the back doors of the ambulance and once Neil was settled he gave Vicky the medical bag containing the antivenene.

'Here you are, lass,' Mac said in his broad Scottish accent. 'Everything you'll be needin'.' He looked down at Neil. 'Well, then, Master Simpson. Been gettin' yourself into a spot of trouble, eh?' Although his words sounded like a reproof, there was a gleam of humour in Mac's eyes. 'You'll be fine, then, lad. Especially with the doc bein' with you so early.'

She prepared the syringe containing the antivenene and swabbed Neil's uninjured arm. 'Ready?' Vicky asked, and Neil bravely nodded. He only gave a slight flinch as the sharp point penetrated his skin. With his best mate beside him he was determined to be as brave as possible, and Vicky was very proud of him.

'Good boy.' Vicky smiled when she was finished, beginning to feel more in command of herself after the stranger's attitude toward her. Vicky packed the things away and glanced at Andrew who was looking a bit exhausted.

'Poor Andrew has had to ride his bike to and from the

road so many times today and you get the royal treatment, being carried on a stretcher,' she said, grinning at Neil. 'Andrew, how about riding in the ambulance with Neil to the hospital? That might make up for the awful time you've had.'

'Yeah? That'd be cool,' Andrew replied, and climbed up to sit beside his friend.

'Neil, I want you to stay in hospital overnight and maybe, if you're good, you can go home tomorrow, but you'll be off school for a few days.'

Neil tried not to look too happy, especially for his friend's sake. The look on Andrew's face said he wished he'd been bitten as well, considering all the attention Neil was getting.

'You'll be able to visit him before school tomorrow, Andrew, and before you know it you'll both be riding around, creating havoc once again,' she told him. 'You've done a good job of helping today and I, for one, am proud of you. I know your parents will be as well.'

'Righty-o, then. Let's get this laddie away to the hospital,' Mac said with a brisk clap of his hands.

'I'll be right behind you,' she told him, and put her medical bag back into her car. As the ambulance wailed its way down the road, Vicky turned to the stranger who was leaning against the Jaguar.

'Nice car,' she told him in an attempt to be polite. 'Here's your bag.'

'Thank you,' he said, and seemed to be waiting for her to say something more.

Biting her tongue so that she wouldn't tell him how arrogant he was, Vicky pasted a smile in place. 'Thank you for your help. Your prompt attention to Neil's situation has probably saved him from a terrible illness.'

He nodded his acceptance of her words, before pulling out a business card. 'My details in case you need to contact me for further information.'

She took the card and, without giving it more than a cursory glance, put it in her pocket, anxious to be gone from his disturbing presence.

He jangled his car keys and held Vicky's gaze for a few timeless moments. 'Would you mind recommending somewhere I could get a healthy bite to eat?'

That was the last thing she'd expected him to say and for a moment she couldn't think straight. Clearing her head, she replied, 'Certainly. The town's coffee-shop sells a wide variety of food and the owner, Faith Jones, is, in my opinion, the best cook in the district. You can't miss it. With today being sunny, there'll be tables and chairs outside and the building is painted bright pink with a big wooden sign saying, "Coffee Shop" hanging from the roof.' She was prattling on but couldn't stop herself.

The stranger's pleasant change in attitude had thrown her off balance. Perhaps he could be halfway decent when he chose. Even with his dark glasses still in place, he was definitely tall, dark and handsome—*and* had that hint of mystery about him.

For the first time since they'd met he gave her a smile. Vicky felt her knees go weak from its effect and instantly knew he had a line of women waiting for him wherever he went. She stepped back awkwardly until she felt the car bonnet behind her. Leaning against it for support, she attempted to collect herself. Desperately, she tried to look away from his handsome face but found herself hypnotised once more. She watched his lips as he spoke.

'With a description such as that, how could I possibly go wrong?'

Come on, Vicky, she urged herself, coherent thoughts would be good at this moment.

'Simple. First, you have to find the town.' Vicky allowed him a small, shy grin. Commanding her legs to support her weight, she brought herself upright and walked to the driver's door of her car. 'Follow me, though, and you'll definitely not go wrong.'

His lips twitched and she realised he'd given her words a double meaning. Good-looking, gorgeous smile and now was he actually displaying signs of a sense of humour? She smiled farewell and gave him a small nod, knowing it would probably be the last time she saw him.

The thought gave her a momentary sense of loss as she watched the way his thighs flexed beneath his trousers as he got into his car. Heart palpitations he might give to every woman he met, but his arrogance and lack of manners would drive her insane, she rationalised as she started the engine.

He was a city doctor through and through, and by the time she'd checked in at the hospital and rushed home to change her clothes for her afternoon appointment, the handsome stranger would be long gone from the district.

When she arrived at the hospital Neil was being well cared for by Nicole Mumford, the director of nursing. Nicole had been in charge since the hospital had opened nearly ten years ago, and since her husband's death a few years previously she had devoted more of her energies and time to both the institution and her patients.

Her appearance was, as usual, neat and tidy, with her crisp uniform and rubber-soled shoes depicting her as the efficient and respected professional she'd always been. Her short dark hair was greying slightly and the sparkle in her eyes told of her natural love for her job.

'He'll be fine, Mrs Simpson,' she was saying to Neil's mother as they talked outside Neil's room. 'The antivenene was given within a good time frame and he's exhibiting no signs or symptoms of distress.' She looked over her shoulder and saw Vicky. 'Isn't that correct, Dr Hansen?'

'Absolutely.' Vicky came to stand by the two women. 'I'd like him to have at least one more injection and to keep

him in overnight for observation. I'll make any other decisions after I've seen him tomorrow morning.' Turning to
Nicole, Vicky dug her hand into her jeans pocket and pulled
out the stranger's business card—forcing herself not to look
at it. He meant nothing to her and, for all his manners and
charm when they'd parted, his previously irritating attitude
still rankled.

'Put this in Neil's file.' She watched as Nicole glanced
at the card with a frown. 'A doctor from the city. Andrew
managed to flag him down first. He had Neil's arm partially
bandaged by the time I arrived. He gave me his card in case
we require any further details.'

Vicky returned her attention to Mrs Simpson. 'Neil was
very brave. Both he and Andrew did all the right things.
Believe me, they've definitely learned their lesson.'

'Let's hope so,' Mrs Simpson said.

Vicky glanced at her watch. 'I'd like to review him now
as I have another engagement this afternoon.' She raked a
hand through her short crop of black hair, thankful she'd
recently had it cut short into a bob. At the moment, though,
it felt like a tangled mess.

'Oh, yes.' Mrs Simpson nodded. 'The auction. What time
does it start?'

'Two o'clock and I still need to get home and change,'
Vicky said despondently. 'It's not something I'm looking
forward to but feel that I must attend.'

'It's quite sad, your sister selling out on you like that. So
many farms around here have been sold lately.' Mrs
Simpson shook her head.

'It's not just the land being sold that upsets me. This is
my heritage. My family history. It's a part of me that's being
unwillingly ripped from my life but my sister refuses to see
things my way. Well, there's not a lot I can do about it now,
other than making sure I get to the town hall on time.' She

shrugged and looked at Nicole. 'Shall we proceed with the review?'

Vicky's home was on the outskirts of town and was generally a fifteen-minute drive from the hospital. Today, she did it in ten! Turning into the dirt driveway that led to the homestead, Vicky wished, not for the first time, that both her brother and sister would reconsider their decisions to sell their portions of land.

Today Leesha's land would go to auction and Jerome had informed her of an interested party willing to go through a private sale. Rushing into the home she'd live in for most of her life, Vicky snatched a quick shower then dressed in one of her business suits. After all, today was business, whether she liked it or not.

The grey suit looked professional and the colour certainly suited her mood. Raking the brush through her hair, she added a flick of blusher and a touch of lipstick, before racing out the door and driving back towards town.

At five minutes to two, she met her closest friend, Mary Jamieson, at the door of the town hall and they quickly took their seats. The atmosphere was stifling. She didn't want to be here…yet she knew it was necessary. After all, she told herself as she took a deep, steadying breath, it wasn't every day that her heritage was sold.

'Will you try and relax?' Mary whispered, placing a hand on Vicky's taut shoulder. 'Every muscle in your body is tense.'

'Oh, no,' Vicky groaned.

'What?' Mary asked, and followed the direction of Vicky's gaze.

'Nigel Fairweather. He came,' Vicky said impatiently, gesturing to a blond-haired man who sat in the front row.

'I thought you said he'd made an offer to Leesha and she'd turned him down?'

'She did. Leesha's husband wanted it to go to auction to see if they could drive the price up further. I knew he'd be here but was hoping against hope that the ground would open up and swallow him before he arrived.'

Mary chuckled but said sincerely, 'I hope, for your sake, Nigel doesn't get it. He's bought too many properties in this area already.'

'He certainly isn't the most welcomed man when he comes to town,' Vicky agreed. 'I still can't believe he actually made me an offer for my third of the property. When I told him I didn't want to sell he thought I was being coy and trying to drive up the price.'

Mary patted her friend's shoulder again. 'Take it easy, Vic. You've got steam coming out of your ears.'

'He just makes me so mad. If only I had the money to buy both Jerome and Leesha out, none of this would be happening.'

'But it is,' Mary said with matter-of-fact logic.

Vicky shuddered. 'I can feel the ground rumbling as Mum turns in her grave.' She reached out a hand and squeezed Mary's. 'Thanks for coming with me today. I really needed you.'

'That's what friends are for. I'm so glad Jeff takes Sundays off and was able to stay with the children. Now, shh. The auctioneer is taking his place.'

The auctioneer walked onto the stage of the McLoughlin Vale town hall. Usually auctions were held at the site in question, but as her sister couldn't be bothered to fly down from Queensland for the event Vicky had pleaded with her not to hold the sale at the farm. Thankfully, on this point, Leesha had conceded.

The auctioneer began pointing his hammer around the room and Vicky was sure he was bouncing bids off the wall, as she'd often heard happened, trying to drive the price up.

Nigel had the final bid and the auctioneer was saying, 'Going once.'

'Please, please, please,' whispered Vicky in desperation. 'Someone else put a bid in.'

As though in answer to her prayer, another man dressed in a business suit in the second row raised his hand to up the bid.

Vicky breathed a sigh of relief and was rewarded with a look of indignation on Nigel's face as he turned to look at the new bidder. The price began to rise again as the two men battled it out.

Every bid Nigel made was raised by his opponent. Vicky's eyes almost popped out of her head at the price the auctioneer was calling out but soon she saw Nigel's shoulders slump in defeat and the hammer fell for the last time. One third of her family property had just been sold to the businessman in the second row.

At least she had the pleasure of seeing Nigel, his face set in anger, storm out of the building, not looking at anyone as he went.

The new owner was congratulated by a few people around him and Vicky slowly released the breath she'd been unconsciously holding. She relaxed in her chair. Nigel hadn't bought the property. She hoped the new owner of Leesha's land wouldn't spoil it the way Nigel would have done. The other properties he'd bought in the district had been stripped of houses, trees and anything else that gave the place character, to be replaced by rows of mass-producing vines.

Slowly people began to leave the room and she watched as a few of the 'suits from the city' celebrated with the new owner of one third of Sheoaks Lane. Although, she amended, the title of Sheoaks Lane now only related to her own property—sandwiched between the others.

'You ready to go?' Mary asked.

'Not just yet,' Vicky replied. 'Strange. When I arrived I couldn't wait to leave and now I don't want to go.'

Mary stood and tucked her shoulder-length blonde hair behind her ears, before absently rubbing a protective hand over her rounded belly, caressing the child beneath. Vicky watched the action with a hint of envy, before turning her eyes back to where the auctioneer was gathering up his papers and leaving the stage.

'Come on, Vic.' When Vicky didn't budge she said, 'I wasn't supposed to tell you but Faith Jones has arranged a little gathering at her place. She called it a "wake" for the loss of your family's property to outsiders. It's in your family's honour and I'm responsible for getting you there.'

'Oh,' Vicky said, touched by the love of the community. 'Then what are we waiting for?' She stood and followed Mary to the door.

'Whoa!' Mary whispered, coming to an abrupt halt. 'Who is that?'

'Who?' Vicky asked, trying to look around her friend.

'The guy in the doorway. I tell you, Vic, if I wasn't a married woman I'd be swooning right now.'

Vicky chuckled for the first time in days. 'You *are* swooning, Mary.' She finally got a glimpse of the man who'd stopped Mary in her tracks.

'It's him,' she whispered, and felt a wave of heat wash over her. She reached out a hand and grabbed the back of a seat to steady herself.

'Who? Do you know him?' Mary asked, noting Vicky's actions before her green eyes danced with surprise.

'Not really.' Vicky quickly let go of the chair and stood up straight. 'I met him this morning.' At Mary's glare, Vicky elaborated. 'He helped out with Neil Simpson and the snake-bite incident I told you about. Remember? That's why I was running late.'

'You didn't say anything about a tall, dark and handsome stranger.'

'I'm trying to put it behind me,' she mumbled, but said more loudly to Mary, 'I gave you the abridged version. Look, can we please just go?'

'Not before I've been introduced,' Mary said stubbornly.

The mystery man was standing by the door and Vicky watched as he shook hands with Fred Durrant, the oldest member of their community. When introduced to Dorothy, Fred's wife, he smiled a heart-melting smile as he raised her frail hand to his lips.

Dorothy blushed and fluttered her eyelashes at him. Vicky couldn't help but be delighted at his attitude. Even though she didn't know his name, she knew he had an old-fashioned charm that would win the heart of every woman he met.

'Come on,' Mary urged. 'Let's go over.'

'Why do I need to go?' Vicky protested, which only increased Mary's smile.

'Because he's the first handsome stranger to walk anywhere near this town who isn't married.'

'Just what I need. An arrogant, opinionated doctor for a husband.'

'Thinking marriage already?' Mary continued to tease. 'He does have you in an tizz, doesn't he?'

'Anyway—' Vicky ignored her friend's comments '—how do you know he's not married?'

'He hasn't got a wedding ring on, silly,' Mary remarked.

'Not all men wear rings. Your Jeff doesn't.'

'Not when he's on the farm, for safety reasons, but he wears it everywhere else.'

Vicky chuckled, seeing the funny side of the scenario. 'You've got a one-track mind, Mary Jamieson.'

'I simply want you to be as happily married as I am.'

'And you think he's the one?' Vicky asked humorously.

'You'll never know if you don't go and say hello.' Mary

hooked her arm through Vicky's and propelled her in the right direction.

'Hello,' Mary said as she stepped alongside Dorothy and thrust her hand towards the stranger. 'I'm Mary Jamieson.'

'Pleased to meet you, Mary.'

Vicky momentarily closed her eyes, remembering the sound of that deep voice. His cologne wound around her senses and began to weave its spell again.

She quickly opened her eyes when she heard him say, 'And if it isn't Dr Hansen.'

'Yes.' Vicky found his smile even more electrifying than before. She turned her focus from his lips to his eyes. The sunglasses were gone. All was now revealed. Blue. His eyes were a startling blue. His gaze was hypnotic and for a moment they simply stood and stared at each other.

'I'm sure she wouldn't mind if you called her Vicky,' Mary supplied when Vicky didn't speak.

Belatedly, Vicky realised he was holding out his hand, and hesitantly put hers into it. If she'd thought her reaction to him before had been disturbing, this was downright dangerous. 'It's a pleasure to meet you, Dr...?' Why was her reply so breathless, so husky?

'Pearce. Steven Pearce.' His fingers curled tightly around her own and gave them a slow squeeze. The blue eyes briefly flicked to her full lips, before returning to her eyes. The action was subtly provocative and Vicky felt her pulse increase. The warm pressure of his hand eased slightly before he pulled his away, leaving her feeling as though she'd lost something.

'You look a little different from our earlier meeting,' he teased, and Vicky felt herself begin to blush.

'Ah, well...it's amazing what a shower and change of clothes can do for a girl,' she responded, her shy smile returning.

LUCY CLARK   23

'How's Neil?'

'Watching television and complaining that he's hungry.'

'A good sign,' he said with a nod.

Where was the man she had encountered only a few hours ago? He was gone, and in his place was this man of charm and elegance. Vicky was baffled, and although she received his attentions she was still quite sceptical.

They fell silent again but were still communicating with their eyes. There was something about Steven Pearce that made her feel decidedly feminine. A feeling she hadn't felt in a very long time.

Mary put her hand out again, breaking the spell. 'It was nice to meet you, Steven.' She turned to her friend. 'We'd better get over to Faith's house before she comes looking for us.'

'Is that Faith Jones?' Steven asked.

'Yes,' Mary answered, as she put her arm through Vicky's.

'In that case, I'll see you there.'

'You've been invited?' Vicky asked incredulously.

'Yes. You sound surprised.'

'No… I just mean…' Vicky floundered, astonished at her own rudeness. 'We're a close-knit community, that's all.'

'And I'm an outsider,' he provided. 'I met Faith in the coffee-shop and she asked me along. Thanks for the directions, by the way. I had no trouble at all, finding the place.'

'I'm glad.' Vicky nodded and forced a smile to try and make amends.

'Would you care to come along with us?' Mary offered.

'Thank you but I have some people I need to see first. It's the big white farmhouse on the corner of the third road on the right. Is that correct?'

Mary laughed. 'I see Faith gave you her usual instructions. That's correct. We'll see you there.' She tugged firmly on Vicky's arm and almost dragged her out of the door.

'Talk about chemistry. You could almost ignite a brush fire with the sparks emanating from the two of you.' Mary fanned her face mockingly as they walked down the street. 'Don't blow this one, Vic.'

'What do you mean?'

Mary shook her head. 'Every time you meet a handsome, intelligent man you erect all sorts of barriers. The few guys you dated during medical school—or at least the ones you eventually told me about—were all pushed away the minute they started to crack and chip their way through the wall surrounding you.'

'I was studying,' Vicky rationalised defensively. 'My mother was depending upon me. Not to mention the rest of this town. It was always known that I would return here to practise.'

'I know,' Mary agreed, 'but that was just an excuse, Vicky. All I'm saying now is don't push Steven Pearce away too quickly.'

'But he doesn't even live here.'

'Excuses already.' Mary threw her hands up in the air in defeat. 'These things can be overcome. Nothing is insurmountable which true love cannot conquer.'

'Your hormones are out of control. I want you to come in for a check-up first thing tomorrow morning,' Vicky said, trying to ignore Mary's words.

'I just don't want you to be unhappy—unmarried.'

Vicky turned to face her friend. 'I'm not married, Mary, because that's what I *choose*. I simply don't have the time for a husband while I'm trying to cope with my workload. I have so many patients in my busy little practice that I'll need to get a partner or locum in soon, not to mention the responsibility of being on the hospital board. I have house calls, hospital rounds and the financial burden of the loan I took to buy the practice in the first place. And to top all that, one third of my family land has been sold from beneath me this afternoon.' Her voice broke near the end of her speech and Mary pulled her into her arms.

'I'm sorry, Vic. I didn't mean to come down hard on you. I know what a strain today has been. You're also right that marriage isn't everyone's idea of happiness, but you forget that I know you too well. We've been friends since kinder-garten and I know you want to get married some day and have a family. It's one of the reasons you've worked so hard to return to Sheoaks Lane—''the perfect place to raise children'', you said. Just don't go fooling yourself that you're happy being free and single because the worst thing you could do right now is kid yourself.'

Mary looked into her friend's pretty face. 'Come on. Let's go and have some of Faith's delicious home-made scones and cream. That's bound to cheer you up.'

Vicky smiled. 'Thanks, Mary.' The words were said softly and with heartfelt sincerity.

CHAPTER TWO

FAITH JONES welcomed them to her home, just as she did everyone she met. It was no wonder she'd invited the handsome Steven Pearce to come along. Faith, now in her late eighties and going as strong as ever, had always appreciated a handsome face. Her husband of sixty-odd years had passed away only a few months previously but Faith's zest for life hadn't diminished.

'I hope you don't mind, dear, that I've invited a few outsiders to join us today. They were in the town coffee-shop, and when I told them of the terrible deed that's been done to you they asked if they could join in to offer their sympathies. Of course, when I was introduced to that lovely Mr Pearce, I simply *had* to invite him as well.'

The fact that Faith had invited outsiders somehow made Vicky feel better about her invitation to Steven Pearce. It was nice of people to commiserate with her, especially when they understood the loss she felt.

The land had been in her family for three generations, all of them dairy farmers. When her father had died at an early age Vicky's mother had been determined to keep his dream alive. She'd managed the farm and the dairy admirably, as well as putting her three children through school. Jerome had won a scholarship to study medicine while Leesha had married and moved to Queensland with her new husband at the age of twenty.

Vicky's desire to become a doctor had pleased her mother and, considering she was the only member of her family to love and adore the country life they'd lived, she'd promised her mother that she would one day practise medicine in McLoughlin Vale.

By the time Vicky had been ready for medical school the farm hadn't been doing so well, but her mother had been determined to pay for her youngest child's tuition. Between the two of them they'd just scraped by, but before Vicky could finish her internship her mother had passed away.

Sheoaks Lane was all she had to remember her by. Jerome and Leesha had willingly given Vicky the homestead and surrounding land, each taking a third on either side. Now they were sacrificing their heritage for monetary gain. She hadn't expected either of them to understand her position and her begging and pleading had fallen on deaf ears.

Raising the money to buy the other two thirds herself had been a far-off dream. There was no way she could afford it, especially after sinking all her savings into purchasing her medical practice.

Vicky was pleased to see the number of locals in the room, and caught Frank Mitchell's eye. He finished his conversation with Fred Durrant and crossed the room to where Vicky stood. As he walked she observed the slight unevenness to his gait, only noticeable to her expert medical eye.

He kissed her cheek and said, 'We're all here for you, girl.' Frank was one of her father's oldest friends and his twinkling blue eyes and oddball humour often reminded her of her father. Indeed, most of the people in the room had known her since she was born.

'Thanks, Frank,' Vicky replied. 'Oh, and don't you dare forget your appointment in my clinic tomorrow.'

'How could I?' he asked, rolling his eyes. 'Mavis still has a go at me for missing my last appointment. Between the two of you I have no hope.'

'If you don't come in for regular check-ups, Frank, that hip replacement will loom closer,' Vicky warned.

'I'll be there,' he assured her. 'Right on time. Now, I hear my great-grandson has been getting into some mischief.'

'Yes,' Vicky replied. 'He and Neil Simpson have been very fortunate, although I would like to ask you to make a bit of a fuss over Andrew for the next few days. Contact your granddaughter and suggest they reward him for his excellent behaviour.'

'He's always been a good lad, young Andrew,' Frank said with pride.

'He kept calm and got help immediately, but once the drama was over, in Andrew's eyes, Neil was the lucky one as I'll be prescribing complete bed rest for him for the entire week—which means no school.'

'Ah,' Frank said with a knowing nod. 'Andrew didn't get bitten, did everything right and Neil is the one who gets time off school.'

'That's the way a twelve-year-old boy would see it.'

'Not to worry, girl. We'll make sure he's fussed over for his heroics.'

'Thanks.'

They stood for a while and watched people coming through the door and being welcomed by Faith. Steven Pearce appeared and raised Faith's hand to his lips in a gentle kiss.

'Knows how to treat the ladies, doesn't he?' Frank murmured.

Vicky agreed. 'He knows darn well these women love the Errol Flynn gesture and are forevermore captivated by him.'

Not that she blamed them, she added silently. He was a very handsome man.

Steven looked casually around the room before his eyes came to rest on hers. They held for a moment and Vicky's stomach churned in anticipation. How could this relative stranger evoke such a torrent of emotions in her? She'd always been proud of her self-control where the opposite sex had been concerned, but Steven Pearce...

Frank, interpreting the glance, quickly excused himself as Steven walked across to where Vicky stood.

'Have you been bad?' he asked, and his teasing smile sent her heart racing.

'No,' she replied automatically as she forced herself to stop focusing on her reaction to him.

'Then why are you stuck in the corner? I thought this gathering was in your family's honour.'

'It is.' She shrugged.

'Then, as the only member of your family here, wouldn't that make you the guest of honour?'

'Perhaps. It depends on how you look at it. Most people here have found themselves in a similar situation—the sale of their family land. So I'd say it's more a gathering of kindred spirits.' She sighed, once again focusing on her present misery.

Steven put his hands into his trouser pockets and inclined his head slightly. 'That land means a lot to you, doesn't it?'

'It did.' She looked down at the empty cup she held. That was how she felt at the moment—empty. 'It doesn't really matter now. What's done is done. I guess I should try and look on the bright side.'

'And that is?'

'That Nigel Fairweather didn't get the property.'

'Nigel Fairweather,' Steven repeated.

'He's a property developer who has bought quite a lot of land in this area over the past few years. He strips the properties of their character, their history and their charm, turning them into row after row of regimented vines.'

Steven frowned. 'I was led to believe McLoughlin Vale was renowned for its fabulous wines.'

'That's correct. Our local winemakers make the most incredible wines, do great trade and bring in tourism.'

'Then what's the problem with Fairweather doing the same?'

'Simple. He's not local. His profits don't come back into the community and with the way he develops the properties he's ruined the ambience the place used to offer.'

'I see.' Steven nodded slowly. 'It's very interesting to hear you say that.'

'Why?' Vicky asked with a teasing smile. 'Considering giving up your day job and moving into the area to plant a vineyard?'

His reply was a laugh that increased the warmth within her. 'The government certainly offers an incentive to do so when you consider that the level of taxation is in favour of the wine producers.'

'That's why Nigel Fairweather has been doing so much buying.'

'From the way you speak of him, I gather you don't care for him very much.'

'What's there to care for? He's simply a city slicker with an eye for opportunity who cares nothing for people or their feelings.'

'He's a businessman,' Steven stated. 'Most successful businessmen turn into billionaires, and billionaires don't care too much for anything or anyone—except the dollar, of course.'

'Know quite a few billionaires, do you?'

Steven laughed again. 'Some days, Vicky, I wish I did.' He gestured at her cup. 'Can I get you another drink?'

'No, thank you.'

'A glass of wine, perhaps?'

'No. I'm on call so alcohol is out of the question.'

'Forgive me for saying so but you really don't look old enough to be a qualified doctor. Although,' he added at her grimace, 'it appears you've been told that before. So exactly how old are you, Dr Hansen?'

'Don't you know it's rude to ask a woman's age, Dr Pearce?'

He leaned a little closer to her, his eyes never leaving hers. 'I'll tell you mine if you'll tell me yours,' he said softly.

She smiled up at him, all too aware of his close proximity. 'I'm twenty-nine.' The three words were said with a breathlessness that Vicky silently cursed. What was it about this man that could rock her foundations? His charm? His charisma? His hypnotic blue eyes that seemed to devour every inch of her?

'You don't look a day over thirty,' he replied and leaned back to gauge her reaction.

Vicky couldn't help it. She looked up at him and laughed. 'You're so full of flattery, Steven. Did you major in it at university?'

'As a matter of fact, no, I didn't. It's a God-given gift.'

Vicky smiled, enjoying his company. 'So aren't you going to tell me your age? After all, fair is fair.'

'I'm thirty-six,' he confessed, and was about to say more when a loud shout stopped him.

'Vicky? Where's Vicky?' Faith's voice called loudly through the house, silencing everyone. Vicky absently thrust her empty cup at Steven and hurried in the direction of Faith's voice.

'It's Mary,' Faith said as she reached for Vicky's arm and pulled her to the bathroom.

Vicky found her friend lying on the floor with her arms clutched around her middle.

'Cramps?' Vicky asked as she touched Mary's forehead. She was very hot.

'Mmm,' Mary groaned in pain.

'Any bleeding?'

'Mmm,' she repeated, her eyes tightly closed, her face distorted in agony.

Vicky snapped the phone off her waistband and pressed a button. 'I'm at Faith's and I need the ambulance here immediately. Mary Jamieson, possible miscarriage.'

'So the ambulance is on its way,' a deep voice commented once Vicky had finished the call. Steven had obviously followed her and Vicky was annoyed at his presumptuous behaviour.

'What gestation is her pregnancy?' Steven enquired as he knelt beside Mary, who was curled in a foetal position.

'Almost sixteen weeks,' she replied as she pulled the hand-towel off the rail and soaked it with cold water. She placed it on Mary's head, trying to cool her down. 'It's all right. I'm here.'

'I'll get hold of Jeff and arrange for someone to take the children,' Faith said, and left them alone.

'If you don't mind, Steven,' Vicky said, without looking at him, her voice quiet so as not to disturb her friend, 'I don't think Mary needs an audience right now.'

'I agree. Frank can keep everyone back. Situations like these can turn from bad to worse within minutes,' he replied in a quiet but authoritative tone.

She reached up, wet the cloth again and reapplied it while Steven checked Mary's pulse.

'Slightly higher than normal but I guess that's to be expected,' he said, and received an acknowledging nod from Vicky. 'How long will it take for the ambulance to get here?'

'A couple of minutes,' Vicky murmured, her concern for her friend increasing. Her concern turned to anxiety as a multitude of scenarios flashed through her mind. What could be wrong?

'Where is he?' No sooner were the words out of her mouth than the bathroom door was opened by Mac.

'Well, Mary, lass,' he drawled, 'let's get ye onto the stretcher and away to hospital.'

As she climbed into the ambulance beside Mary, Vicky turned to Steven. 'Thanks for your help. If things had gone wrong, it was reassuring to know I had someone else there.'

He nodded at her words and stood back for Mac to shut the doors. Within a matter of minutes they were pulling into the hospital grounds and Mary was taken to the emergency treatment room.

'There you are, Steve.' David Malcolm crossed the hospital foyer and extended his hand to his friend. 'I'm amazed at how I turn my back to finalise the sale and you manage to disappear, absorbed into this community in under an hour,' the blond-haired managing director of the Sharlock Wine Company said.

Steven gave David's hand a hearty shake. 'I try.' He grinned. 'And may I congratulate you once again on your brilliant tactics in that auction room. The way you played Fairweather was like a maestro violinist in a symphony orchestra.'

'Yes, I was rather good, wasn't I?' David replied bashfully. 'Listen, I just wanted to let you know, the papers are all signed, sealed, delivered.'

'Great.' Steven nodded his head slowly.

'I'll have work crews in immediately to renovate that old cottage on the property and then you can move in, although why you'd want to move from Adelaide to the country is beyond me.'

'You'd never understand,' Steven replied. 'When will the vine-planting begin?'

'In another two to three weeks. We have to move fast as spring is the season to get the soil prepared and the vines organised. Hey,' David added as an afterthought, 'did you meet Jerome's sister? What's her name?'

'Vicky.'

'That's it. Did you have a chance to talk to her?'

'Yes and no.'

'Meaning?'

'I've spoken to her but not about the sale of her land.' Steven rocked back on his heels, a glint of determination in his eyes. 'I'll need to employ different tactics with her. She has a stronger attachment to the land than we anticipated.'

'Tactics? Such as…?'

'Ah… I have a few things up my sleeve,' Steven said with a knowing smile.

'Watch it, mate,' David replied with a grin. 'You could be letting yourself in for more than you bargained for. Remember that redhead in Naracoorte? One kiss, and as far as her old man was concerned that was as good as an engagement ring.'

'Now, now. You blow everything out of proportion.' Steven chuckled. 'But I can assure you, this time will be different.'

'Why? Isn't Vicky Hansen much of a looker?'

Steven slowly exhaled. 'Looker? She's stunning,' he stated.

David gave him a pat on the back. 'Good luck, my friend. It looks as though you're going to need it.' He glanced down at his watch. 'I'm due back in the city by five, so I'd better get going. Are you planning to…stay the night?' He grinned wolfishly.

'No, I'm not,' Steven said emphatically. 'I have a full elective surgery list starting early tomorrow morning.'

'Keep me posted.' David waved as he headed for the door.

Shaking his head, Steven turned his attention to the task at hand—finding out where Vicky was and checking on Mary's condition. He headed down the corridor to the nurses' station.

'May I help you?' Nicole asked.

'Yes. I'm Steven Pearce.'

*   *   *

Jeff rushed in, desperate to see his wife. 'What's happening, Vicky?' The expression on his face was a mixture of anxiety and fear.

'Mary's lost a lot of blood, Jeff, but it seems to be stopping and the cramping has gone. It's still touch and go.'

'She had back pain last night. We thought it was just the baby "adjusting",' Jeff said as he tenderly stroked his wife's forehead. 'She had the same back pain with Anita so we didn't give it another thought.'

Vicky looked at her friend. 'I'd like you to stay in overnight for a few tests. I'll do an ultrasound to check on the baby but bed rest is paramount. I know you had some bleeding around the fifth week and maybe that was an early warning sign. I'm sorry I can't give you a definite diagnosis but after the ultrasound I'll have a better idea.'

'When will you do that?' Jeff asked anxiously.

'Immediately.' As the words left her lips, Lydia, the hospital's midwife, wheeled in the portable ultrasound equipment, as well as a foetal heart monitor.

Vicky reached for her friend's hand and gave it a squeeze. 'I know this pregnancy has been different from the others and that you haven't been too well but, regardless of what happens, we're all here for you.'

'The children,' Mary said, and Jeff quickly shushed her.

'Faith is taking care of everything. She was planning on taking them to her place for dinner and, if necessary, a sleep-over. She'll make sure Tom gets to school on time.'

Mary visibly relaxed at this news and closed her eyes.

Vicky switched the foetal heart monitor on and tried to locate the baby's heartbeat. She held her breath and moved the monitor again. Nothing!

'What is it?' Jeff asked, and Mary's eyes snapped open.

Vicky tried a different angle. Again—nothing!

'Vicky?' Jeff said, his voice cracking slightly, 'what's happening?'

'I can't find the baby's heartbeat. Switch the ultrasound monitor on, Lydia,' Vicky said briskly, and held out her hand for the small paddle that would enable the picture to be displayed.

What she saw brought tears to her eyes. The baby's spine was malformed and the greater part of the brain was absent. If only she'd done a scan earlier when the initial bleeding had occurred but, she reasoned, a lot of women had minor spotting in the first few weeks. Mary had admitted to having spotting when pregnant with Anita so both had dismissed the notion that something could be wrong.

'What is it?' Mary asked softly as she watched Vicky's expression. Vicky turned the monitor around so that Mary could see what was wrong.

'The baby's dead. It's what we term anencephalic, which means that most of the brain and the bones at the rear of the skull aren't developed.'

Silence filled the room as they all looked at the image on the monitor.

'How long has the baby been dead?' Mary whispered, reaching out a hand to touch the small screen.

'Not long. When you had that first initial cramp at Faith's, that's when it probably happened.'

'Isn't there something we can do?' Jeff asked.

'No.' Vicky turned to face her friends. 'I'm so sorry. With the main part of the brain missing, the baby would have had no chance of life.'

The silence intensified. Regardless of the fact that Mary was her closest friend, Vicky needed to remain professional and calm to help them through this ordeal. 'I'll need to induce labour as soon as possible.'

'Yes,' Mary whispered, gathering the mental strength which Vicky had seen on many occasions. 'I'd like to be awake for the birth of my third child, if that's possible.'

Vicky nodded.

'I want to see the baby, Vic, even though it's dead. I will be able to see my darling, won't I?'

'Yes,' Vicky replied. 'We'll take a photo as well so you can explain it to the children.'

'I'd like that,' Mary said, and looked to her husband. 'You'll be there, won't you?'

'Of course, honey,' he said, and kissed her.

Vicky turned away from the emotional scene. Why, oh, why did this have to happen? Especially to Mary. All those years of medical training and she was still unable to help her friend. She concentrated on packing up the ultrasound equipment and wheeled it out of the room, giving the Jamiesons time to digest the depressing and heart-breaking news.

'Vicky?' Nicole took the trolley from her. 'What's wrong?'

'Anencephalic,' Vicky said, and closed her eyes at Nicole's quick intake of breath.

'Dead?'

'Yes.'

Nicole ran a hand over her crisp uniform. 'I'll arrange a theatre immediately and contact Emma. When she arrives I'll send her in to the doctor's tearoom, which is where you'll be relaxing.'

'Yes, Sister,' Vicky replied meekly, and received a satisfied nod from her friend. Emma Travis was the hospital's anaesthetist. She was slightly smaller than Vicky and had mousy brown hair. She was also a little older than Vicky and had been married for two months.

If Vicky thought the community was close-knit, it was nothing compared to the thirty-bed hospital they ran. It was staffed by well-trained personnel from around the district, who were dedicated to providing the best treatment and care for all patients.

The smell of freshly brewed coffee met her as she pushed

open the door to the doctor's tearoom. She managed to raise a slight smile. Trust Nicole to think of everything. She poured herself a cup, before turning around to sit in one of the comfortable lounges.

'Oh!' She sucked in her breath as she noticed Steven Pearce sitting quietly, a journal in his lap as he intently watched her. 'Don't do that!' Vicky snapped, looking down at the hot cup of coffee she was holding. 'I might have scalded myself.'

'I'm sorry,' he said, but his smile belied his words. 'Nicole told me this would be the best place to wait for you.'

'Oh, she did, did she?' Vicky muttered as she put her cup on the table and planted both hands on her hips. 'Well, she should have mentioned it, instead of assisting you in scaring the living daylights out of me.' She turned on her heel and headed for the door.

Steven moved like lightning and was blocking her exit before she could blink. 'Don't get mad at Nicole,' he said, placing a hand on her shoulder. 'I told her not say anything. I'm sorry, Vicky.' His eyes met hers and this time the apology was sincere. 'Please, sit down and enjoy your coffee. No doubt you need it.'

'Why do you say that?' she asked as she capitulated and sat down.

'You don't look too happy.'

'I'm not. The baby's dead. Anencephalic.'

'I see,' he said.

'No, you don't,' Vicky responded, fire leaping into her eyes. 'She had spotting earlier on and I didn't do a scan. She's carried this baby to almost half-term and now I have to take it away from her.' She hit the armrest of the chair in anger. 'Why didn't I do the scan? Why didn't I read the signs? Why didn't I do further tests? Why didn't Mary tell me about her cramps and backaches?'

Silently, Steven sat beside her, letting her talk. 'She's my best friend,' she told him. 'I have all this medical training and I still can't save her child.'

'You're human, Vicky.' His deep voice washed over her and he squeezed her hand. 'You may have medical training and expertise but you're still human. Doctors aren't miracle-workers. We all have to be reminded of that from time to time.'

Vicky leaned closer to him and he placed his arm about her shoulders, offering her comfort. She buried her head against his chest, listening to the steady beat of his heart. The tears that had been threatening to fall disappeared in his embrace.

Then realisation dawned on her. She was comfortable within Steven Pearce's arms and had absolutely no desire to move.

Mary was given an epidural and labour was induced with an intravenous injection of oxytocin. After just an hour of pushing, a baby boy was delivered, no bigger than Vicky's gloved hand. Placed in a sterile drape, she showed him to Mary and Jeff before Lydia, the midwife, took a polaroid photograph. Then Vicky carefully handed him to his parents.

'He's so tiny and fragile,' Mary whispered as tears rolled down her cheeks.

'He has the same nose as Tom,' Jeff observed.

'Look at his fingernails—there's so much detail.'

As they discussed their son, Vicky stood by, feeling helpless yet knowing this delivery had been the only outcome. 'He's both of you,' she said. 'What are you going to name him?'

Mary looked up at her husband, who also had tears in his eyes. 'Stuart,' Jeff said firmly. 'It was the name we'd decided on at the beginning of the pregnancy.'

'He looks so peaceful, like he's sleeping.' Mary sighed then gave her son a kiss and said, 'Goodbye, Stuart. We love you.' Then she gave him back to Lydia who took Stuart to perform further tests.

With one of the other nurses monitoring Mary's condition, Vicky excused herself. 'I'll be back in a moment,' she said, and walked out of the room, unable to witness the heart-breaking scene any longer. She ripped off her gloves, gown and mask, and furiously scrubbed at her hands.

As far as days went, she'd definitely had better. Snake bites, the sale of her family land and now the loss of a child. And not just any child but her best friend's. Try and look for the silver lining, her mother had always told her. Where was it today? she thought.

What about Steven Pearce? The question popped into her head unwillingly. What about him? Was *he* a silver lining? Admittedly, being able to confide in another doctor had been wonderful. To feel his arms tenderly around her had been incredible, awakening a desire she'd never experienced before.

She turned off the tap, telling herself not to get sidetracked into thinking about a man who was just passing through town. She still had work to do.

After seeing Mary settled into a private room, Vicky went to her office to complete the mountain of paperwork the termination had generated.

It was difficult to concentrate on the words she needed to write, her concern for Mary's health foremost in her mind. Physically Mary would make a complete recovery but her mental and emotional health wouldn't be so easily restored. Should she refer her to a psychologist? She would have to monitor the situation closely and watch for signs of post-natal depression. Regardless of when in a pregnancy a woman gave birth, the side effects were the same.

Vicky forced herself to concentrate on the work at hand.

The sooner she finished, the sooner she could visit Mary and check her progress. An hour later Vicky put her pen to rest, before going to Mary's room. Lydia and Nicole had been keeping a very close eye on their patient.

When she entered the room, Lydia stood up and left them alone. Mary's blonde hair was splayed out on the pillows as she gazed out of the window. She looked so…sad.

'Hi,' Vicky said softly as she crossed to the bedside and rested one hand on Mary's forehead, checking her temperature. 'Where's Jeff?' she asked as she quickly scanned the observation chart.

'He's gone to speak to the children. We think they should be told as soon as possible. I don't know if Anita will understand completely, being only three, but the fact that the new baby has died will sink in with Thomas.' Mary was silent for a while and Vicky didn't press her.

'I've just been lying here since he left, thankful that we already have two healthy and beautiful children.'

Vicky grasped her hand reassuringly but didn't speak.

'I remember holding him. So small and delicate. I saw his head, Vicky. I know you had him in a drape but I saw the deformed skull. I know that even if I'd carried him to full term, he still wouldn't have survived.' Tears began to slide down her cheeks.

Vicky reached her free hand out for a tissue from the box nearby and gently dabbed at Mary's eyes. 'I wish there was something more I could have done. There were tests I should have performed earlier…but the outcome still would have been the same.' She finally allowed the tears to flow down her own cheeks. At this moment she wasn't Mary's doctor, she was Mary's best friend, and they embraced, sharing their grief.

It was a while later, with puffy eyes, red noses and a bin full of used tissues, that Vicky sat down.

'Well, I don't know about you,' she said, 'but I feel a bit better.'

'Me, too,' Mary responded with her first real smile since the tragedy.

The door to the room opened and Jeff walked in. Seeing the smile on his wife's face, a mirrored one on Vicky's, he felt a whole lot better. He pointed to the bin. 'Been keeping the tissue companies in business again, ladies?'

Mary held out her arms to her husband.

'I'll leave you two alone.' Vicky stood. 'But there are a few things I wanted to ask you both. If it's all right with you, I'd be more than willing to take care of the burial arrangements. I've already filled in the paperwork from the medical angle so there won't be much more to complete. Besides, I have the necessary forms in my office.'

Mary and Jeff looked at each other and Vicky envied the silent communication they shared. 'Thank you,' Mary said. 'We'd appreciate it.'

'Consider it done. I'd like you to stay in at least overnight and I'll assess your condition in the morning.'

'Thanks, Vicky. For everything.'

'Ditto,' Vicky replied. 'Ah!' She raised a hand to her ear. 'Who is that I can hear outside the door, impatient to see their mother?'

'You brought them with you?' Mary smiled up at her husband.

'Just try and keep them away!' he remarked.

'Open the door, Vicky,' Mary said.

Vicky did as she was asked, and Thomas and Anita came bursting into the previously serene room, filling it with colour and animation in the way only children could. She smiled at the family before her, knowing that the two children would be the best medicine for both Mary and Jeff.

Slipping out of the room, Vicky left the Jamieson family to become reacquainted. Before returning to her office to complete her paperwork, she stopped in to see Neil Simpson. 'I can see I've no need to ask how you're feeling,' she said as she observed him. He was sitting up in bed, a large tray of food in front of him, watching the television.

'Yep. I'm feeling just fine,' he replied as he swallowed a mouthful.

'I'm glad to hear it. I presume your mum's gone home?'

'Yep,' he said again, as he filled his mouth.

Vicky checked his observation chart and was very pleased with the results. It appeared that Master Simpson would suffer no ill effects from his adventure with the brown snake.

'I see you've had your blood test,' she said as she hung the chart back at the end of his bed. 'We should have the results through tomorrow morning so I'll be back to see you then. In the meantime, don't eat too much or you'll get a tummy ache, and I'm sure Sister Mumford will make sure the television is off at a reasonable hour.'

Neil nodded. 'She promised Mum to turn it off at eight o'clock sharp.'

Vicky laughed. 'Then enjoy it while you can. Goodnight, Neil. Sleep well.'

When she returned to her office she found a few extra papers Nicole had placed in her in-basket which required her attention, and once they'd been dealt with Vicky filled in the forms relating to Stuart Jamieson.

Because he had only been of sixteen weeks gestation, Vicky knew it was the responsibility of the parents to take care of the burial and associated costs. The government would only accept legal recognition of the baby when it was twenty weeks or more.

After contacting the local undertaker and making arrangements with the morgue, Vicky pushed the papers to the side of her desk and threw her pen down as though burned by the contact. She rubbed wearily at her eyes, willing the ache in her head to disappear.

'You look as though you've been put through the wringer.'

Vicky looked up into the blue eyes of Steven Pearce. 'You *still* here?'

He walked towards her desk, never breaking eye contact. 'Do you always say the first thing that pops into your head?'

'Generally,' she admitted with a rueful smile. 'I'm sorry, Steven. You're just the last person I expected to see. I thought you'd gone hours ago.'

He looked briefly at his watch, then back at her. He leaned over and put both hands on her desk, bringing his face within centimetres of her own. 'I'll let you have some free advice.' His tone was soft and intimate and Vicky watched the way his tongue darted between his teeth as he spoke. 'I'm not that easy to get rid of.'

'Like a bad smell?' she enquired innocently, and his rich chuckle fell over her like a warm blanket.

'No. I think I should warn you that when I want something...or someone...' He paused and let his eyes rest on hers for a moment. 'I pursue them—with a passion.'

Vicky swallowed nervously as he brought his face even closer to hers. 'And...wh-what is it you want now?'

'Dinner, with a beautiful woman and a glass of local red wine.' His breath fanned her cheeks. She forced herself to lean back in her chair, attempting to put more distance between them.

'Well,' she said, her voice cracking on the single word. She cleared her throat and raised her eyes to meet his. 'If it's the company of a beautiful woman you're after, I'd be happy to recommend some names. Although I'm sure you have a string of them a mile long back in the city.'

He straightened, threw back his head and laughed. 'Victoria Hansen, you're priceless.' He came around to her side of the desk and held out a hand to her. 'It's *your* company I desire. I've talked the owner of your exquisite hotel into packing a take-away dinner for two. Tonight's menu is—'

'Roast beef, crisp baked potatoes, carrots, peas, onions and gravy. I know,' she replied. 'He serves that every Sunday evening. I often get take-away.'

Steven's shoulders slumped a little and he hung his head in mock dejection. 'I can see my efforts to impress you have failed.' He was silent for a moment. 'What if I told you that I also had—'

'Fresh black forest cake for dessert?' she interrupted.

'Does the guy serve the same thing *every* week?' Steven asked, raising his arms in disbelief.

Vicky laughed as she collected her bag and the papers for Nicole. 'Welcome to the country, Dr Pearce. Now, if you'll kindly step outside, I can lock my office.'

'Does this mean you'll accept my offer?'

'Considering all the trouble you've gone to, it seems a shame not to. Just tell me, where are you planning on serving this feast?'

He cleared his throat and mumbled something.

'Pardon?' Vicky asked, a hand around her ear.

'At your place.'

'Oh, so now you're inviting yourself back to my home? Very smooth. Is this the way it works in the city? Supply a girl with food and expect her to reheat it? Then leave her with the dishes afterwards, all so you can feed your stomach in relative comfort without a gaggle of people around?' She headed down the corridor, not waiting for his answer. After the strenuous day she welcomed a bit of light relief, and if it came in the unlikely form of Steven Pearce then so be it.

'Goodnight, Nicole,' she said, and handed over the paperwork. 'I won't disturb Mary again but call me if necessary.'

'Yes, Doctor…and goodnight, Mr Pearce,' Nicole added

with a smile as he followed Vicky out of the hospital with a farewell wave.

'You know, we'll probably be considered an item,' Vicky told him as she walked to her car, her smile still in place.

'That doesn't seem to bother you very much,' he observed.

'Why should it?' she asked as she opened the car door and put her bag inside. 'An eligible young bachelor comes into town for the day, buys me dinner and then whisks himself away. If you ever return, *you're* the one who will be hounded if you so much as speak to another single woman.'

'I see.' He mulled over her words. He took a step closer to where she stood by the open car door. He gave her a nod and then reached out a hand to brush some hair out of her eyes. 'So, does that mean you don't mind doing the dishes?'

'I have a dishwasher,' she replied, the humour of the situation disappearing into thin air. If he was still willing to come to her home and have dinner after what she'd just told him, the man had guts. Being hounded by this community, that was not something to relish. Then again, she acknowledged, he might never return to this part of the country.

She ran her tongue over her lips and looked into his eyes. If she'd thought them hypnotic before, it was nothing compared to how he was making her feel now. The atmosphere between them was charged as his fingers gently trailed down her cheek, then dropped to his side.

Taking a step backwards, he broke the mood and gave her a stern look. 'You know, Vicky, you shouldn't leave your car unlocked. It might have been stolen or vandalised.'

Giving her head a little shake at his change in attitude, Vicky looked around at her car. The navy blue, four-wheel-drive station wagon was very dirty. She gave him a smile. 'You've been living in the city too long. Besides, I couldn't lock my car even if I'd wanted to.'

'Why?'

'Because I arrived at the hospital by ambulance, remember?'

'Then how…?'

Vicky shrugged. 'Mac, the ambulance driver, or Nicole probably arranged for someone to get my keys from my bag, collect my car from the town hall car park, where I'd left it when I attended the auction, and drive it to the hospital. See.' She pointed inside. 'The keys are in the ignition. All ready for me to jump in and go home to a scrumptious meal with a handsome bachelor.' She hesitated, then frowned. 'You are single, aren't you?'

Steven laughed. 'Yes. Yes, I am and I presume you are, too. Otherwise, you'd be the one hung, drawn and quartered by not only the community but your husband as well.'

'True,' she replied.

'So, how far is your place from here?'

'About fifteen minutes.'

'Let's get going, then. I'll follow you.'

'Good idea. Especially considering I know where I'm going.' She looked at his Jaguar, nice and shiny in the car park, and shook her head. 'Perhaps it might take us *twenty* minutes as we'll need to go the long way around—your snazzy sports car won't be able to handle the dirt roads.'

He acknowledged her comments with a slight incline of his head. 'How considerate of you.'

Vicky giggled as she climbed into her car. He shut her door, before walking to his Jaguar. 'Mary is going to be so proud of me,' she told her steering-wheel as she started the engine.

CHAPTER THREE

VICKY opened the back door and entered the renovated wooden homestead which had been her childhood home. A sense of warmth enveloped her immediately. Even though her mother was no longer there to welcome her, she only had to look around for happy memories to come flooding back.

She left the door open for Steven and walked through to the kitchen. Turning on the light, she extracted plates and glasses, smiling to herself as she set the small, square kitchen table. On the short drive home, she'd considered whether it was better to eat in the large, spacious dining room, where she and her family had shared their evening meal, or in the kitchen where she now ate by herself.

The old kitchen was a comfy room and, although it could be thought intimate, Vicky was determined to ignore the interpretation Steven might put on it. There would be wine, yes, but no candles.

There was a knock at the door and Vicky called out, 'Come on in.' His footsteps sounded on the wooden floorboards of the hallway, then stopped as he stood, cardboard box in hand, in the kitchen doorway.

'Just put it down on the bench,' Vicky said as she continued to place the cutlery on the table. When she had finished, she checked inside the box. 'We'll have to take the food out of the foil trays so it can be reheated in the microwave.' She immediately began transferring the food onto plates. 'The wine rack is over there.' She gestured with her head, her hands still busy. 'You have the choice of a lovely local selection of traditional reds—as per your request.

Corkscrew is in the top drawer here.' She inclined her head towards the cabinet of drawers.

'Any preference?' he asked, going to inspect her wines.

'No. You choose.' Vicky covered the food so it wouldn't dry out and placed the plates on the two-tiered microwave rack and set them to reheat.

Steven selected the wine, uncorked it and set it on the table, then turned to watch Vicky. His intense gaze followed her as she collected the serviettes and salt and pepper. She wondered if he'd guessed how uncertain she was about having him in her home—alone, dinner for two. Glancing at the table, she dismissed the intimate setting it evoked—even without the candles.

Raising her gaze to meet his, she found him smiling at her. 'This meal was supposed to relax you.' He took a few steps closer. 'Not make you even more nervous of me.'

'I'm not nervous,' she replied, a little too quickly. He was standing directly in front of her now and reached for her hand.

'Does my presence disturb you?'

Vicky lowered her eyes for a moment and was just about to look at him again when the microwave beeped. She jerked her hand out of his and turned away.

'Saved by the bell,' he remarked as she gathered a cloth to remove the warmed plates. Ignoring him, she concentrated on not burning herself as she uncovered the food, before carrying it to the table.

'Shall we eat before it gets cold?' she suggested, and sat down, watching him pour the wine.

'I'll let you off the hook—for now,' he said mockingly as he sat down opposite her, 'although I won't let you evade the question forever.'

'I've already forgotten what it was.' Vicky busied herself with her serviette, unable to meet his gaze.

'Don't worry. I'll remind you—one way or another. Besides, at the moment I think I can guess whether or not my presence disturbs you.' He chuckled as he raised his glass to her. 'Here's to good company, good food and a pleasant evening, getting to know each other.'

Vicky raised her glass but didn't reply, although she did sip from her glass, thereby acknowledging his toast.

While they ate, Steven was the perfect dinner companion. He had Vicky laughing as he recounted stories from his childhood.

'My sisters once had a humdinger of a party when my parents were on the other side of Melbourne at a wedding. They were due to stay overnight but Dad ate something that didn't agree with him and was quite ill. Luckily for them, Mum called ahead to tell us about the change in plans.' Steven chuckled at the memory.

'They had the house empty of people and completely clean within an hour. I took photographs and was able to blackmail them for years.'

'I gather you didn't help?'

'No. I was extremely put out that at the very mature age of ten they hadn't let me invite any of my own friends.'

'When did you move to Adelaide?'

'Almost sixteen years ago.'

'And the rest of your family?' Vicky enquired innocently.

'My sister is here and my parents still live in Melbourne.' He paused for a moment before adding, 'My eldest sister, Jill, died nearly twenty years ago.'

'I'm sorry.' Vicky automatically reached out a hand to touch his.

'It's not your fault. She was a doctor, working in Africa. The entire village was involved in a massacre and only one person survived. He is now, as a matter of fact, my brother-in-law and has been happily married to Kathryn for the past nine years.' His face brightened as he spoke of his sister. 'They're both doctors and work at the children's hospital in the city. However, Kathryn will be taking some time off very soon because, after nearly four years under *in vitro* fertilisation treatment, they're expecting their first child in a couple of months.'

Vicky smiled. 'They sound very happy.'

'They are.' He dabbed his serviette over his mouth. 'But enough about me.' He gave her an intense look and curled his fingers around hers. 'I want to hear all about Victoria Hansen.'

She looked down at their entwined fingers then back to his eyes. He was making her nervous again and she jerked her hand away as though he'd burned her. Rising to her feet, she began clearing away the empty plates.

'They always do fantastic meals at the hotel, don't you agree?' she asked, not brave enough to look at him. She concentrated on carefully rinsing the plates and stacking them ever so neatly into the dishwasher.

'Yes,' he agreed, and smiled indulgently at her. Vicky knew he was well aware of how uneasy he made her feel. How unsettling his dynamic presence was to her. He helped her clear away the rest of the paraphernalia, and before she could ask, he'd filled the kettle and switched it on.

'Coffee sounds good. Thanks for asking,' he joked as he watched her flit around the kitchen like a moth near a flame. At his words she stopped briefly and risked a glance in his direction. However, the grin on his face told her he was teasing.

Knowing her stalling tactics couldn't last for too much longer, Vicky decided to give up. She had no objection to telling him about herself and her family. Her objections were to the intimacy of their situation.

In the hospital car park she'd been certain she could handle it but, knowing that even now the community would be gossiping about the dashing Steven Pearce having a quiet intimate dinner with the local doctor, it was more than she was willing to handle.

Her clinic tomorrow would be full of oh-so-innocent questions from the people who had watched her grow up and counted her as one of their own, thereby giving them the right, as far as they were concerned, to pry into her personal affairs.

And where would the dashing Dr Pearce be by then? Back safely at his residence in town. She scowled at him as he leaned casually against her cupboards, his arms folded across his chest.

'Is that look meant for me or have your thoughts taken you elsewhere?' he drawled, and Vicky coloured. Releasing a sigh, she gave up on the emotions fighting inside her and shook her head.

'I'm sorry, Steven. I thought I'd be able to handle the intimacy of having dinner with a man but you have no idea what small country town gossip can be like.'

'I thought you said I was the one who would be hung, drawn and quartered for leaving you in the lurch?'

She smiled. 'You still will be but until then I'll have to put up with the same questions from each patient until you return. *If* you return,' she amended. 'Getting to know me is all well and good but...' She trailed off, not quite sure exactly what to say to him.

He unfolded his arms and stood up straight. In a few short strides he was standing in front of her. 'If you prefer that I leave now I will but, regardless of what the community might say or speculate, I *will* be back. That you can count on. For the moment, all I'd like to do is get to know you. No strings attached.' He turned his winning smile on her. 'Just friends.'

Vicky returned his smile with a shy one of hers. 'Friends,' she repeated. He held out his hand to her and she firmly placed hers within it. The next thing she knew, she was drawn against his chest and enveloped in a warm and comforting hug.

Just when she thought she had him figured out, he went and did something like this. She caught her breath as she remembered the sensations of being held in the same position earlier that afternoon—the scent of his aftershave, the feel of his cotton shirt against her cheek and the warmth of his flesh beneath it. She felt a shudder ripple through her and closed her eyes.

Regardless of what she knew and didn't know about Steven Pearce, of one thing she was certain—the physical attraction she felt for him was unlike *any* she'd ever experienced. She cleared her throat and tried to concentrate on rational thoughts.

'So, do you always hug your…um…friends this way?'

'Always,' his voice rumbled deeply, and she felt it vibrate through her body. The kettle began to whistle, before switching itself off. She felt his arms begin to relax and realised that, although she'd rather stay in his embrace, it was her cue to pull away.

'There always seems to be a buzzer or a bell that interrupts us,' he remarked as she placed coffee cups on the bench. 'Do you have any more programmed to go off?'

She smiled at him, amazed to realise she felt more relaxed after their embrace. 'No. I guess tonight I've been lucky. Why don't you get the black forest cake out while I make the coffee? How do you take it?' He watched as she spooned instant granules into the cups. 'I'm sorry I can't offer you *real* coffee but I'm afraid my coffee-pot broke.'

'I take milk, no sugar.'

'Sweet enough, eh?' she joked, and he smiled.

'So, when you do get around to buying a coffee-pot, will it be a copper one?'

Vicky laughed, amazed they were on the same wavelength. 'I want a proper cup of coffee from a proper copper coffee-pot,' she said, recalling the childhood tongue-twister.

'That's the one. Kathryn always loved tongue twisters and would try them out on me, considering I was younger, more vulnerable and generally couldn't say things correctly.'

'Older siblings.' Vicky chuckled. 'I'm sure they were born to tease us younger ones.'

'Is that something we have in common? We're both the youngest?' He collected the dessert and followed her into the cosy family room.

'Yes,' she replied, setting the cups down.

Books lined the walls and photographs graced the mantelpiece above the open fireplace. The worn easy chair with a footstool was obviously where Vicky spent a lot of her time as various medical journals were strewn on the floor around it.

'I'm sorry about the mess,' she apologised, gathering up the articles.

'Don't apologise. Come and sit over here with me— friend.' He emphasised the last word, then patted the lounge cushion next to him.

Vicky did as he asked. Steven took her hand in his and she tingled at the touch. 'You're a very demonstrative person, aren't you?'

'Why is it that when you say it like that it comes out as an accusation? Yes, I am an...affectionate person. Does it bother you?'

'Yes and no,' she replied honestly. 'I hardly know you but I feel...something between us. I've tried to ignore it, as you've guessed, and only succeeded in making a fool of myself.'

'I don't think you've been foolish at all, Vicky. So, why don't you to tell me about yourself?'

'What do you want to know?' Vicky asked.

'How long have you lived in this community? When did

you complete your medical training?' His voice lowered to a soft whisper. 'Share your memories of your parents and the good times you had.'

Vicky looked at him for a long moment and realised that he understood her loss. After all, he'd told her about the tragic loss of his sister and she could sense that he still felt it very deeply.

'You want the Vicky Hansen story? All right, but if you start dozing off, I'll nudge you.'

Between bites of delicious cake, she told him about her childhood in the town and the fun times she'd shared with Jerome and Leesha. 'Neither of them were comfortable, living in such a close community. Leesha used to say she couldn't sneeze without the whole town discussing it. I, on the other hand, loved the community atmosphere.

'When I left to do my medical training, I'd generally be home for weekends, helping mum out with the dairy. Then, as the medical training became more intense, I pined for home and promised myself over and over that one day I'd set up my practice here and return for good.'

'Which is what you've done,' Steven remarked. 'I admire people with definite goals and dreams, who aren't afraid to put in the blood, sweat and tears to make them become a reality.'

'I only bought the practice six months ago. It's taken every penny I have. Although, with what's been happening recently, I might have done things differently.'

'Such as?'

'Well, Sheoaks Lane. I thought my siblings might have been a little bit more patient and given me time to get finance organised before they sold, but I was wrong. Then there's Nigel Fairweather, hounding me about my portion of the land. I just don't understand why Sheoaks Lane is so attractive to someone like Nigel and those others at the auction.'

Steven pondered her words for a moment. 'It could be because the Mediterranean conditions, which grapevines respond to so well here, are more pronounced on this side of the valley. At least,' he added, 'that's what I overheard at the auction.'

'Really? I knew about the Mediterranean conditions in this area,' Vicky responded, 'but I didn't realise they extended this far inland.'

'What about the practice? Would you still have brought it, knowing about the land sales?'

Vicky sighed. 'I suppose I would have. Dr Loveday was ready to retire and handed everything over, lock stock and barrel. He still comes in one day a week to continue seeing a few patients but people have been very supportive and willing for me to handle their needs. My only problem now is that business seems to have boomed and I find myself with more patients than I can handle.'

'Time to look for a locum?'

'Soon. I can still handle things for a while but not for too much longer. Besides the practice, I have responsibilities at the hospital. Not that I'm complaining,' Vicky said quickly, and Steven smiled.

'I didn't think for a moment that you were.'

'Today was so hard for me. I keep going over and over in my mind Mary's earlier check-ups.'

He took her hands in his. 'Don't blame yourself, Vicky. We've all lost patients at one time or another. It's the downside of being a doctor.'

Steven placed his arms around her and she welcomed the touch. They sat like that for quite some time before Vicky felt the tensions of her day begin to slip away in his embrace. With a sigh, she finally looked up at him. 'Thank you,' she whispered, realising just how close they were. 'It's such a relief to confide in another doctor.'

As she spoke, Vicky found it difficult not to focus on his

mouth. Her eyes flicked up to his and then back to his mouth again, wondering what it would be like to feel the pressure of his lips against her own. Her entire body sprang to life and tingled at the thought.

Her mouth went dry and she swallowed, before darting her tongue out to wet her lips. After doing this, she realised Steven might think her provocative. Was that a bad thing? If the truth be told, she was growing desperate for him to kiss her.

'The pleasure,' he said as be brought his hands up to frame her face, 'is all mine.' He drew her closer and slowly lowered his head to press his lips softly against her own. Vicky's breath caught in her throat at the brief touch before she kissed him back the same way.

With agonising slowness, Steven's mouth teased hers. Once…twice…three times. Each time the pressure became more insistent, more demanding. Vicky's lips parted, allowing him to seek out more of her hidden sweetness.

His kisses sought and searched, exploring her mouth and allowing her access to his. Vicky couldn't control her responses and, giving up all attempts to do so, allowed his expertise to guide her.

When Steven's hands slid from her face and down her neck, she found it impossible to control the shiver of excitement that coursed through her. When his hand brushed tentatively around the side of her breast, the moan that escaped her lips was one of pure pleasure.

As though this sound was what he'd been waiting for, Steven gathered her closer, lifting her to sit on his lap—his mouth never breaking contact.

Vicky leaned against him, wrapping one arm about his neck and plunging the other into his thick, dark hair. *Never* had she been kissed like this before. They were two separate entities, wanting and needing in equal amounts. Passion fused them together, before raging higher and stronger at every new stroke of his tongue. Vicky knew this was pure torment…and she never wanted it to end.

The old grandfather clock in the hall chimed eleven. At the noise Steven reluctantly broke away but continued to hold her to him as they both caught their breath. 'I didn't realise it was so late.' He lifted her chin with his hand so their eyes could meet. They stared at each other for a moment, both still dazed and surprised at how a few simple kisses had spun them out of control. 'I need to get going,' he said, almost apologetically. 'I also have a clinic tomorrow morning and, considering the hour-long drive I have ahead of me, I'd better be leaving.'

Vicky eased herself from him, beginning to feel self-conscious about her ardent responses. Apparently, Steven felt no such awkwardness as he took her hand, planted one more fleeting kiss on her lips and led them from the room.

'Walk me to the car,' he said as he released her hand briefly to put his jacket on.

Like a docile puppy, she followed him. At his car, Vicky managed to regain a modicum of sense. 'Thank you…for tonight. Dinner was great and…I…had a…good time.'

'*Good?*' he asked in disbelief. 'Is that the best you can do?'

'All right,' she relented with a smile. 'Perhaps it was a bit better than good.'

'I think we need to have another…session, which will hopefully improve your choice of adjectives.' Steven raised Vicky's hand to his lips. 'You take care.'

She nodded. 'Drive carefully.'

'I will.' He climbed into his car and rolled down the window. 'Come here.' He beckoned with his finger. When she bent her head close to his, he captured her lips once more, as though he were reluctant to depart.

When he finally drew away, Vicky's knees were about

ready to collapse on her. His kisses were so…perfect for her.

'Go inside,' he urged as he started the engine. 'The wind's turned cool and I don't want to be held responsible for the town's doctor getting sick.'

She smiled at his words, feeling warmed by his sensitivity, then raised her hand as she said the typical Australian farewell. 'See you later, Steven.'

'You will, Vicky. Trust me—you will.'

CHAPTER FOUR

THE next morning Vicky was up early and at the hospital to check on Mary and Neil, before beginning her clinic.

She went to see Neil first, knowing the gossip of the evening meal with Steven would have already reached Mary and that her friend would insist on hearing all the juicy details.

When she walked into the male ward she crossed to the foot of Neil's bed and shook her head. 'Have you slept at all since I last saw you?'

'Yep,' he said.

'You're in exactly the same position, Neil Simpson. Sitting up, eating, with the television on.' She laughed. 'I can see you're taking advantage of this situation while you can. Tell me, did Sister Mumford forget to turn that contraption off last night?'

'No. At eight o'clock sharp, right in the middle of something I was watching, she came in and switched it off, telling me that if I turned it on when she walked out of the room she'd ring my mum.' He gave Vicky a puzzled frown. 'She wouldn't *really* have called my mum, would she?'

'She most certainly would have,' Vicky replied, trying to keep a straight face. 'I presume you played it safe and didn't risk turning the TV back on again.'

'You bet I played it safe.' He nodded vigorously. 'Mum says I've given her enough of a scare and a lot of extra work, what with her having to come to the hospital to see me and then probably having me home from school for this week. The last thing I want to do right now is make her even angrier.'

'Good thinking.'

'Do I really get the whole week off school?' Neil's eyes were wide with delight at the prospect.

'I'd like you to rest at home, in bed or on the couch, for this week, yes—but,' she added, 'I've asked Sister Mumford to contact your teacher. She'll send your school work home so you don't miss out on anything.'

'Aw, do you have to, Dr Hansen?' He groaned. Again, Vicky struggled to keep her expression serious.

'This isn't a holiday, Neil. If I hadn't been in the area to help you straight away, you might have been extremely ill and possibly even had to go to an Adelaide hospital for further treatment. Then what would your mum have had to say?'

Neil gulped.

'I want you to take it easy this week. No running around, no visiting your friends, no riding your bike—nothing! I want you to stay as quiet as possible the whole week and I'll be around on Friday to check on you. I also want you to do exactly what your mum and dad tell you. You'll have your school work to concentrate on for most of the day, and if you do it all with little fuss I'm sure your mum will let you watch some TV.'

'Sounds like good advice,' Nicole said as she bustled into the ward. 'Your mum just phoned to say she'll be around to see you once she's dropped the other kids off at school.' She looked at Vicky. 'I should have the blood test results phoned through from the pathology lab in Adelaide by midday.'

'Good. Let me know what they are, but from the looks of things I think Neil will be able to go home some time—'

'After lunch?' he prompted, then had the grace to look a little sheepish. 'It's just that the food's really great here.'

Vicky laughed. 'For your mother's sake, yes, you can go

home after lunch. That's one less meal she'll have to provide for you.'

'Anything else, Doctor?' Nicole asked.

'No. Tell Mrs Simpson I'll call around on Friday to check on him but, apart from that, a very quiet week.' She waggled her finger at her young patient for emphasis. 'Now, I think I'll quickly see my other patient before I tackle my busy clinic. Enjoy your morning, Neil.'

'I will.' Then, with all the good manners his mother had instilled into him, he said, 'Thank you for your help, Dr Hansen.'

'You're welcome,' she replied and left him in Nicole's care.

Mary's room was in the next corridor. 'I hear you had a relatively comfortable night,' Vicky said in her best 'doctor' voice as she strolled into the room.

'I'm so glad you're here.' Mary shifted herself amongst the pillows. 'Nicole won't give me a definite answer as to when I can go home. She said it was up to you.'

'It is.'

'Great—so does that mean I can go?'

Vicky scanned Mary's chart then held it to her chest and regarded her patient carefully. 'Just because I'm your best friend, it doesn't mean you can push me around, Mary Jamieson.'

'Oh, yes, it does,' she replied, settling back again. 'I'm missing Jeff and the kids.'

'I know.' Vicky took another look at the chart, which showed that everything was normal. 'You've made a good recovery and I realise the best thing for you right now is to be with your family. Yes, you can go home, but you must promise me…' she pointed her finger at Mary '…to take it slowly. I'll organise for meals to be dropped in for the next few days. No house-cleaning, no cooking, no helping Jeff with the farm and no lifting the children. If I find you've done otherwise, I'll re-admit you until you can learn to be-have.'

'Yes, Doctor,' Mary said meekly, but a smile lit her face. 'So, now you've finished discussing me, let's discuss you.'

'What about me?' Vicky asked, knowing the inquisition was about to begin.

Mary scoffed.

'Don't play the innocent with me. I heard you had a din-ner guest last night.'

'I did.'

'Turned your happy little niche upside down, did he?'

'We had dinner—that's all.' She was silent for a moment then shrugged nonchalantly and said, 'It was…pleasant.' She was sure Steven would have cringed at that description, especially after he'd rejected 'good'.

'Oh, please,' Mary scolded. 'First you play innocent, then you insult me. Come on, Vicky, remember who you're talk-ing to.'

Vicky held her breath, before sinking down onto the bed. 'Mary, it was scary and wonderful and romantic and…'

The twinkle in Mary's eyes said it all. 'He's managed to pry open the door you've kept locked for so long. Good for him—and good for *you*. When will you be seeing him again?'

'I don't know.' Her voice actually broke on the last word and Vicky sighed heavily. 'He said he'd be back but…'

Mary clapped her hands. 'This is so romantic. I can't wait to tell Jeff.'

'I'm sure he already knows. In fact, I'm sure there isn't a single person in this community who doesn't know. I bet half of them stayed up to see what time his car drove through the main street, checking that he left at a respectable hour.'

'And did he?'

'Around eleven.' Vicky shrugged. 'I'm not looking forward to the clinic today. Every patient will want to play twenty questions and I'll be running late all day long.'

'I'm sure they won't mind.'

'Oh, no.' She threw her hands in the air. '*They* won't mind at all, so long as their curiosity is satisfied.' She grasped her friend's hand and shook her head uncertainly. 'I hope I can handle the gossip. Last night I thought I could handle being alone with a man in my house but it was…' Vicky slouched dejectedly and dropped Mary's hand. 'I guess I'll just take things as they come. For now.' She stood. 'I'd better get to the clinic before they break down my door.'

'Come around when you finish tonight and I promise to commiserate with you,' Mary suggested. 'I presume Faith will be providing the meal for us as she always likes to get in first. That means there'll be plenty of food so please stop by when you've finished.'

'OK,' Vicky agreed. 'Don't wait for me—just save me some food and I'll reheat it. Chances are, I'll probably be late.'

'Well, youngster,' Frank Mitchell said loudly as he walked into Vicky's clinic room, his grey, bushy eyebrows raised in interest. 'Been doing some entertaining, I hear.'

'Yes, Frank. Take off your coat and roll up your sleeve so I can check your blood pressure.' Vicky reached for the sphygmomanometer, before fitting the cuff around his arm. Putting her stethoscope in place, she pumped the cuff up then slowly released the pressure, watching the indicator closely.

'Good.' She undid the cuff and packed it away again. 'One-twenty over eighty.' She returned to the other side of her desk and picked up her pen to make notes. 'Do you need a repeat prescription for your medication?'

'Yes,' Frank replied absently. 'So, what's he like? I only

saw him from a distance at Faith's place yesterday. Rather tall, isn't he?'

'Yes, Frank,' Vicky replied matter-of-factly, not looking at her patient and concentrating on writing out his script. 'Everything else been normal since your last check-up?'

'Right as rain, girl. I was told your young man ordered two meals. Did it taste as good as usual?'

'Yes.' Vicky ignored his remark about her 'young man'. 'Now that I'm assured your heart is still beating, we'll check your hip. Have you been doing the exercises I showed you?' She finally raised her eyes to meet his. His grin was wide and Vicky groaned inwardly.

Her prediction was coming true. Today was going to be even longer than yesterday, if that was at all possible. Frank was only her first patient and Trudy, her receptionist, had told her the clinic was full.

She placed her pen back onto the desk. 'OK. Let's get it out of the way. The meal was great, as usual. Steven Pearce was good company and, yes, I'd like to see him again. Happy now?'

'You bet I am.'

'Good. Now, can I please have a closer look at your hip? Drop your trousers and get up onto the examination couch.'

Frank let out a deep, rumbling laugh. 'If that's your bed-side manner, I have a feeling Mr Pearce will be coming back for more.'

'Thank you, Frank.' Vicky ignored his comments and proceeded with her examination. When she had finished she helped Frank off the couch and started to write some notes while he got dressed.

She waited until he was seated opposite her again, before saying, 'I'd really prefer an orthopaedic surgeon to look at that hip.'

'But—'

'I know,' she interrupted. 'You've been doing your exercises.'

'You said use it or lose it. I've been doing them, every night. I promise.'

'I believe you, Frank, but I'm not talking about surgery—yet. This problem has been brewing for a number of years and you will eventually need a total hip replacement. Hopefully, we can stall for a bit longer but it is slowly getting worse.'

'Stalling sounds good to me.'

Vicky smiled. 'I'd still like you to see a specialist. It would be wonderful if we had one assigned to the hospital but, unfortunately, most orthopods prefer the comfort of their private clinics and private hospitals to do their consulting. I'll look into it and see what I can arrange for you.'

'Thanks.'

'Don't thank me yet. The next thing you need to do is get some of that hard labour taken off your shoulders or, to be more precise, off your hip.'

'But, girl—'

'No, Frank. I understand farming is your life and I'm not telling you to quit. I'm asking you to be sensible about this. You're almost eighty-three and you're not as young as you used to be.'

'Tell me about it,' he mumbled, but nodded.

'Any activity that gives you the slightest twinge of pain, I want you to delegate to one of your farmhands. That's what they're there for.'

Frank levelled a piercing stare at her but the twitch of his lips belied his seriousness. 'What if I have trouble when I'm being a considerate husband to Mavis? Do I get one of the farmhands to take over *that* job?'

Vicky tried to keep her face straight. 'I think you should discuss that with Mavis. After all, some of your farmhands are very handsome young men.'

'Victoria Hansen,' he spluttered with mock indignation, 'your mother would turn in her grave if she heard you saying such things.'

Vicky let the laughter bubble out. 'I sincerely doubt it. I'll set up the specialist appointment as soon as I can. Won't be for another few months as their waiting lists are usually a mile long.'

'Sounds fine to me.' Frank stood. 'Just one last thing before I go.'

'Yes?'

'Enjoy yourself with this Steven Pearce. I know everyone out there…' he pointed to her door '…is eager to find out what happened between the two of you, myself included, but remember, girl, it's only because we love you.'

'I know,' she replied, and went around the desk to hug him. 'Thanks, Frank.'

'It's the least I can do for my old mate's little girl. Your daddy would have been right proud of you and we all knew your mother thought you the best daughter in the world.'

'Frank,' Vicky said warningly as she stepped back, 'don't *you* start getting emotional on me. I count on you to be my rock.'

'I'm there, girl. We all are.' He gave her a nod, before walking out the door. Vicky sat back in her chair and buried her head in her hands. They all cared—too much sometimes. Even more so since her mother's death.

Her intercom buzzed and Trudy said, 'Ready for the next patient?'

Vicky depressed the button. 'Let the interrogation begin.'

The following day, her clinic wasn't nearly as hectic. Most of her inquisitive patients had already come, so even though the questions still flowed they weren't as constant.

She'd been correct when she'd warned Steven that they would be linked as an item. Although most of the townsfolk were happy for her to have a man in her life, they'd promised to tar and feather him if he hurt *their* little girl.

Strange, she mused, that one dinner was interpreted as having a man in her life. She wondered what would happen when he stayed the night? Shotguns at her door the next morning?

Vicky chuckled to herself, then realised the path her thoughts were taking. *When* he stayed the night? She hadn't heard from him for two days—not that she'd expected to, she rationalised. She was getting too caught up in the town's fantasy.

Glancing down at her watch, she noted that if she didn't get a move on she'd be late for the board meeting at the hospital. At least today's clinic had finished on time.

She gathered the necessary papers and drove the short block to the hospital.

'Afternoon, Brian.' She greeted the physician who serviced the hospital and was also the chairman. Placing her papers on the table, she slumped gratefully into a chair.

'How's life been treating you, Vic?'

'Not too bad. How's Annie? Feeling better?'

He nodded. 'She's almost at the end of it. I know the saying is that doctors and nurses make the worst patients but I think that should be changed to doctor's wives making the worst patients.'

Vicky smiled. 'Has she been driving you crazy?'

'Yes. ''Sympathy, Brian. I need sympathy,'' she keeps telling me. It was a chest infection and I know the coughing drives her crazy but that's no reason for her to drive *me* crazy. I offered our daughter all the money in the world if she'd come home for a few weeks and nurse her mother. She turned me down!'

'Hard to believe.' Vicky laughed, knowing he was joking. Brian and Annie Phillips had been married for thirty years and loved each other dearly.

The other board members arrived and the meeting began. When all the general business was out of the way, Brian introduced a special item.

'I know it's not on the agenda but I have some good news concerning our need for an orthopaedic specialist. I've been negotiating for a few months with a colleague of mine, doing everything in my power to convince him to expand his practice and start a clinic here. One half-day per week to begin with and then we can take it from there.' He smiled excitedly at each member.

'Fantastic!' Vicky applauded, similar sentiments being echoed by others. 'Why didn't you tell us before?'

'I wanted to wait until it was signed, sealed and delivered. I've prepared a dossier on our new surgeon for your perusal.' Brian handed out papers to each member. 'Hopefully, within the next half-hour, we can discuss his qualifications, experience and suitability to this position, then cast our votes as to his acceptance into this hospital.'

'Great work, Brian. I think a note of thanks should be entered into the minutes regarding Brian's tireless efforts in bringing this to fruition,' Vicky suggested.

'Agreed.'

'Seconded.'

The motion of thanks was passed. All eight people who made up the hospital board were beaming from ear to ear.

'So don't keep us in suspense any longer.' Vicky flicked open the documents before her. 'Who is he?'

She saw the name in black and white at the same moment Brian said it. 'Mr Steven Pearce.'

Vicky looked at the chairman in astonishment, her mouth wide open in amazement. She blinked three times before his words began to register and then quickly closed her mouth...but was too late. Everyone had seen her reaction. The lady sitting next to her patted her arm.

'There you go, dear. Plenty of opportunity to catch yourself a husband now,' Janet whispered in her ear.

Vicky glared at her and said briskly, 'I'm not out to *catch* a husband, Janet.' The second the words were out of her mouth she instantly regretted them. 'I'm sorry, Janet. I'm just a bit on edge.'

Janet smiled again. 'It's all right, Vicky. No need to apologise. My Derek had me in a right royal uproar before we even started dating, and that was over forty years ago.'

'But he's not… We're not…' Vicky tried emphatically to deny anything but wasn't quite sure exactly what she was denying. The fact remained—Steven Pearce *was* coming to her hospital on a permanent basis. The documents in front of her were proof of that. He *would* be in the district again and he'd obviously known it the other night but had conveniently forgotten to mention it to her.

'If you'd like to read the documents I've prepared, we'll get down to business,' Brian said. Vicky tried hard to concentrate as she read through Steven's impressive credentials. He currently held the position of Senior Consultant at the major teaching hospital in Adelaide, as well as conducting extensive research into various aspects of orthopaedic surgery. His presentations on this subject had won him awards at numerous world conferences. Vicky's respect for him grew even more.

'Now, if we could get down to discussing these matters,' Brian announced, 'we can then proceed to a vote.'

There wasn't too much discussion as everyone agreed the hospital needed an orthopaedic surgeon and Steven Pearce's credentials were exceptional. A unanimous vote was reached in favour of appointing Mr Steven Pearce.

'He's agreed to hold his first clinic at this hospital next week,' Brian said, 'so things are definitely moving ahead. That's it. Thank you for your time.'

Vicky gathered up her papers and walked out before anyone could corner her and start asking personal questions. She was mad at herself for allowing her flustered emotions to be displayed in front of her colleagues. Where was her professionalism? How could she have openly gaped at Brian when he'd announced Steven's name? Were her feelings written across her face for the world to see?

'Vicky.'

She thrust the papers into her car and waited for Brian to cross to her. 'I'm sorry I couldn't warn you, but Steven had specifically asked me not to.'

'How long have you known him?'

'Quite a few years. The last time I was in the city he mentioned an interest in the southern region of the state. I wasn't about to look a gift horse in the mouth and let him go, so I blatantly set out to help him decide this area could do with his services. He'll also be working a few days per week at Victor Harbour hospital, as well as keeping his private clinic and operating list going in the city. Quite a hefty workload but he's got the stamina and the ability to see it through.'

'Was that why he was here on the weekend? To give the place the once-over?'

'I guess so. He'd mentioned he had some business to conduct down this way and decided to stop in and check things out.' Brian smiled at her. 'I think you might have actually helped him to finally decide.'

'Me?'

'You welcomed him to your home and showed him what country hospitality is all about.'

'That's hogwash, Brian, and you know it.'

He shrugged but decided not to pursue the matter further. 'He had a good talk with Nicole regarding hospital matters on Sunday and phoned me on Monday morning to accept the offer. He'll be down this weekend to get things set up.'

'Thanks for the warning,' Vicky muttered. 'I'd better go.'

'Again, Vicky…' He placed a hand on her arm. 'I'm sorry I couldn't warn you.'

Vicky dredged up a smile for him. 'Don't worry. I'm sure things will work themselves out. And it is fantastic that we'll finally have an orthopaedic surgeon for this district. I've got a string of people ready to refer to him.'

'I'm sure he'd be pleased to hear that.'

Vicky said goodnight, then climbed into her car and drove home. The swine, she thought. The lying, deceiving swine. She'd felt something special between them on Sunday evening—a strong physical attraction, which was why she'd been fighting it. The memory of his kisses still lingered foremost in her mind and she'd lain awake in bed for the past two nights, imagining more.

Not tonight, she told herself sternly as she walked into the cool house. Switching on the gas heater, which would warm the place within minutes, Vicky paced the room. In all fairness to Steven, he hadn't lied, she reminded herself. He'd simply omitted some basic facts about himself. The first one—that he was thinking of moving here. The second—that he was a qualified orthopaedic surgeon. He was a 'Mr', not just a 'Dr'.

Surely, as they'd sat and talked about themselves at her kitchen table, those would have been small titbits of information he'd felt he could share with her. Granting him the fact that he might have wanted to surprise her about moving to the area, she thought it odd that he hadn't mentioned his speciality, though, if he had, she knew the first words out of her mouth would have been, 'Fancy that. You're just the kind of man we're looking for.'

Vicky could see his reasoning but didn't agree with it. She hadn't expected him to confess his innermost secrets to her but those general topics had been carefully avoided. It made her wonder what else he had conveniently forgotten to mention.

*   *   *

On Friday morning, Vicky was coming in from collecting the eggs from her chicken run located at the rear of the property when she saw, out of the corner of her eye, a vehicle on what had been Leesha's land. From where she stood, she could see around half of Jerome's land and most of Leesha's.

As Vicky watched in disbelief, a white van pulled up outside the small one-bedroom cottage that stood in the corner of the property. The last time she'd been to the cottage it had been in need of extensive renovations as no one had lived there for over fifty years.

As children, they'd tidied it up a little and used it as a cubby house, but the teasets had been long since removed from the premises and Vicky hadn't been over there since her return. After all, it was Leesha's land, and Leesha had sold it to invest the money in her husband's firm. Whatever that van was doing on the land, it was none of her business.

She started back towards the house, concentrating on controlling her emotions at someone else moving onto what had always been Hansen land. She placed the egg basket on the bench with a thud and the top egg toppled over and smashed on the floor.

Vicky looked down at the broken egg—white and yolk mixing together amongst the bits of hard shell. That was how she felt. Her hard shell had been cracked open and emotions were starting to spill out.

The phone shrilled to life, snapping her out of her reverie. Lifting the cordless phone off the table where she'd left it, she said, 'Vicky Hansen.' Then she started to clear up the mess with the phone to her ear.

'Vicky—it's Molly. It's happened again.' Molly was the local vet and had recently experienced a break-in at her surgery. Stolen drugs had been the result.

'When?'

'It had to have been last night. Not the surgery this time

but my bag. I went to check over my supplies and the vial in my bag is empty.'

'My clinic doesn't start until this afternoon.' Vicky sighed, knowing her one morning off was going to be filled yet again. 'How are you situated?'

'I've got an hour to spare. I have to be out at the Mitchell farm by ten-thirty.'

'Great. I presume you've called Daniel so I'll meet you at your place in around fifteen minutes.' Vicky ended the call and finished cleaning up the mess. Quickly changing into navy trousers and a white shirt, she collected her jacket and bag, before heading to her car.

Molly's farm wasn't far and Daniel's police car was there when she arrived. He was still quite new to the area, having moved here with his wife and two-year-old daughter only a year ago, but the family had fitted in perfectly. The policeman was well over six feet tall, with ginger hair and moustache, and was very dedicated to his profession.

'This is the second time,' Molly told Daniel as he took notes. She shook her head in disgust, her shoulder-length blonde hair tied back in a ponytail. 'Five days ago drugs were taken from my surgery, as you know. I've had the place locked up as tight as a drum, not that it wasn't before.'

'If people want to get in,' Daniel pointed out, 'they always find a way—especially if it's a junkie we're dealing with, which is where all the evidence is pointing. Any drugs missing from your premises or the hospital, Vicky?'

'Not that I know of. You might want to speak with the anaesthetist, Emma Travis. I can give you her contact numbers but ketamine isn't generally used on humans any more, mainly animals.'

'The vial was a one hundred milligram bottle and, as I said, it was in my bag but empty.' Molly handed a handkerchief, containing the vial, to Daniel. 'Naturally, you'd find my fingerprints and hopefully you'll be able to pick up some others.'

'I hope so, too,' Daniel said, but didn't sound hopeful at all. 'How could someone have got into your bag? Do you leave it in your surgery? In your car? In the house?' he asked.

Vicky listened as Molly retraced her steps for the past few days, unsure of exactly when it could have happened. 'I rarely have it out of my sight but those instances I gave you are the only ones I can think of. My car, as with most other people's, isn't locked, but again my bag isn't left in the car either. The house is relatively secure but someone could have broken in last night while I was sleeping and taken the ketamine then. Although I haven't noticed any signs of forced entry.'

Vicky looked at the top of the vial. 'They've used a syringe to withdraw the liquid, which means it probably went directly into the user's arm.' She shook her head.

'What?' Daniel asked. 'I know little about this drug, except what Molly told me the first time it happened.'

'Ketamine is also available in powder form and is usually snorted. It gives hallucinations for around twenty to forty minutes. If injected, it lasts a lot longer and can cause users to fall into what we term a "K-hole".'

'What's a K-hole?' Daniel didn't look up from his notebook as he furiously took the information down.

'The drug doesn't make you feel happy or elated like Ecstasy or other designer drugs. Instead, you space out and hallucinate. Falling into a K-hole is similar to a full-blown panic attack. Accelerated heartbeat, deep and fast breathing and sweats. People on ketamine have no idea what is happening around them, often thinking they're walking on the moon when they're really walking on a busy highway.'

'So it's obviously very popular in the city. I guess the first place to start is with any newcomers to the district. I'll send out information to other police stations. Would you both let your colleagues know to keep a lookout?' Daniel requested.

He looked at Vicky. 'If someone were to come into your clinic or the hospital in a K-hole, would the symptoms be recognisable?'

'If it's something we know to be on the lookout for. Generally the person would be brought in by a friend as they'd be too spaced out to realise what was happening.'

'Thanks, Vicky. I'll be around at the hospital later today and I'll check with Emma. For now...' he turned to Molly '...I'll have a look around here to see if I can see any signs of forced entry.'

Vicky drove back towards her own farm. The driveway to Leesha's property came before hers and on impulse she turned into it. Although she didn't like the fact that the land had been sold, she was eager to get a closer look at the man from the auction who had purchased it. After all, she reasoned as the car bumped its way over the dirt track, she was just being neighbourly.

'Hi,' she said as she alighted from her car. 'Just moving into the area?' She walked over and held out her hand to the two men, who were having a cigarette and leaning against the van.

They shook her hand in greeting before one of them said, 'We're just the electricians.'

'Mind if I take a look?' She gestured to the cottage which looked like new from the outside. She obviously hadn't noticed that the new owners had been renovating the place during the past week.

When the men squirmed a bit she pointed to the tip of her roof, which could be seen from where they stood. 'I live there, which is why I thought I'd drop by and introduce myself to my new neighbours.'

'Sure.' They shrugged and relaxed as though her explanation made sense.

Vicky went inside and took stock of her surroundings. Renovations were definitely in progress. The kitchen, which was against the far wall, was being upgraded with the latest equipment. She looked around the corner where the bathroom, which had previously held a large enamel tub, was undergoing extensive alterations. A shower cubicle was being inserted, as well as an inside toilet. She smiled. Apparently, her new neighbour didn't care much for the outhouse.

A four-poster bed took up most of the main room, which was bedroom and lounge room rolled into one. Other than that, boxes were littered everywhere.

'Well, well,' a familiar voice said from the doorway. 'Fancy finding you here *and* in my bedroom. Curiosity got the better of you, Vicky?'

She turned—slowly—and looked into the deep blue eyes of Steven Pearce. 'What?' She gave him a quizzical look, hoping his words would penetrate the haze his appearance had evoked.

'There's still quite a bit of work to be done, as you can see.' He motioned around the room, then leaned casually against the doorframe.

'*You* live here?' she asked with incredulity.

CHAPTER FIVE

'Yes,' he replied. 'Considering I'm the new orthopaedic surgeon for the district, I thought it advantageous that I find myself somewhere to live. Fortunately for me, the managing director of the Sharlock Wine Company decided he wanted someone staying in this cottage. Couldn't have worked out better. Although,' he added, looking around the room, 'the renovations aren't moving along as quickly as he'd anticipated.'

Vicky blinked, trying to clear the haze in her mind. During the past week she had been dreading and wishing for Steven's return, but this was not how she had envisioned it.

'You *know* the managing director of the Sharlock Wine Company?' She'd heard on the local grapevine who the new owners of Leesha's land were so the name wasn't completely foreign to her.

'Yes. I know David very well.' He raised an enquiring eyebrow. 'Is that a problem?'

'I guess not,' she replied, her lips pursed tightly, her back rigid. She looked at him for a few moments. His hands were in his jeans pockets, his chin jutting out and she wondered if there was more to his living arrangements than he was admitting.

The fact that he was connected, even through friendship, with the very people who had bought her family land weighed heavily on Vicky's heart. It was as though he were siding with the enemy. It was ridiculous, she knew, to be cross at him just for being friends with the managing director of the Sharlock Wine Company, but she couldn't help it. Vicky knew her body language belied her words and she hoped Steven realised that.

'Actually, I'm pleased to find you here.' He took his hands out of his pockets and took a step closer to her.

His words and movements made her cautious. 'Oh?'

'Yes. I have a favour to ask. As you can see, the plumbing…' he indicated the kitchen and bathroom '…is still being done and the council won't permit habitation. So I've decided to stay at your place for the next few weeks.'

'Oh, you have, have you?' Vicky could feel her temper begin to rise.

'It will take at least that long for the job to be completed and to get the council's stamp of approval, and so on.' He shrugged and spread his arms out wide, as though it were out of his hands. 'Please?' he added in a gentler tone. Then he smiled like a mischievous schoolboy, his eyes twinkling with merriment. 'I promise I'll be good.'

Vicky stood in the centre of the room, trying to get a fix on her emotions. She was dumbfounded at his audacity in inviting himself as her house guest, after informing her that he consorted with the enemy. But that smile of his was creating more havoc than she liked.

He'd just promised to be good—but good at *what*? She already knew he was a fantastic kisser and that he could accelerate her heartbeat with a simple look. All sorts of hot and steamy images flashed through Vicky's mind. She forced herself to push them aside. Now was not the time or place to let her fantasies about Steven Pearce intrude.

A few weeks of having Steven in her house? Would she survive living in such close quarters with him? The fact that she was attracted to him, which he no doubt knew, could be her undoing. And what about the community? If she thought the gossip had been bad when he'd come to dinner, she could imagine what it would be like if he stayed for a few days.

What do you have to lose? A small voice inside her head enquired. The townsfolk had already matched them as a couple so why shouldn't she just go for it? After all, she was a single woman and he was a single man. *Very* single! Why not let nature take its course?

'Vicky.' Steven's voice brought her back from her reverie, his charming smile still in place. 'I also promise no hanky-panky.' He raised his fingers to his forehead in the Scout salute.

Why, when he promised this, did she feel so…disappointed? When she didn't reply, he gave her a wolfish grin.

'Not unless you *want* some hanky-panky?' His eyes were alight with humour and Vicky turned on her heel and marched out of the door, hoping he hadn't seen the tell-tale blush revealing that was *exactly* what her thoughts had been.

'I've got my bags in the car,' he said. She'd had no idea he'd followed her and was startled at his words. Vicky stopped dead in her tracks, and Steven cannoned into her.

'Sorry,' he drawled. His hand came around her waist to steady her and she turned to face him.

Looking into his blue eyes, Vicky's embarrassment dissolved. The electrically charged atmosphere surrounding them was all she could concentrate on. His hand remained on her waist as he returned her gaze.

Steven wasn't holding her captive so she was free to turn and walk away, but she couldn't. She'd missed him and Vicky knew her feelings were evident in her face.

'Come here,' he murmured, before lowering his head, his lips claiming hers in a gentle kiss.

Vicky closed her eyes, giving herself up to the moment, remembering what it was like to be cradled against him as his other hand tangled in the back of her hair, drawing her closer to him.

The pressure from his lips was everything she'd dreamed

over the past week. His scent, the way he felt as she let her hands slide up his chest, feeling the contours of his body beneath his cotton polo shirt, was all a distant memory being brought back to life once more.

When he finally drew away Vicky slowly opened her eyes, not at all eager to break the contact completely. Resting her head on his chest, she listened to his heartbeat. They stood together for a few more minutes before a voice behind them said, 'Wish my wife would welcome me home like that.'

Vicky sprang out of Steven's hold and looked around to see the electricians watching them closely with great amusement.

Feeling her initial embarrassment return, Vicky fished her car keys out from her pocket and stormed over to her car, without looking at any of the men.

Climbing in, she revved the engine and put it into reverse, grinding the gears as she did so. She knew Steven would follow but she wasn't going to hang around, giving the men more opportunities to laugh at her. Thank goodness they weren't local tradesmen.

Vicky drove on autopilot to her property and drove her car around the back of the homestead to the open garage.

She decided to wait for Steven and was leaning against the car when a red Range Rover came up the drive and parked next to hers.

'What happened to the Jaguar?' she asked as he climbed out.

'I took your advice and decided that if I was going to be out in the country, a more suitable vehicle was necessary. But never fear,' he added, 'the Jaguar is safe back in the city—although that might be a contradiction in terms.' He smiled.

Vicky returned his smile, feeling a little more at ease now

that they didn't have an audience. She gestured to the door. 'Come on in.'

She could feel his eyes watching the sway of her body as she walked ahead of him into the house and through to the kitchen. Vicky switched the kettle on and asked, 'Coffee?'

'That reminds me.' Steven turned and walked out of the house, leaving her standing helplessly in the kitchen awaiting his return. He reappeared and, after dumping a large canvas bag onto the floor, he bent to unzip it. The way those denim jeans hugged his firm, muscled thighs had Vicky almost hyperventilating. She ran her tongue over her lips and was caught in the act as Steven straightened. He smiled but didn't comment. Instead, he held out a beautifully gift-wrapped box.

'What's this?' She blushed but accepted the present.

'I like real coffee,' he said and a few moments later she laughed as she pulled a proper copper coffee pot from the box.

'Thank you.' She ran a finger down the length of the pot, touched by his gesture. He *had* thought about her during the past week and the knowledge made her very happy.

'Your *real* coffee might have to wait as I don't have any coffee beans in the house. I'll go to the store and see what they have in.'

'Freshly ground.' Steven produced a long, gold-coloured pack of coffee.

'You weren't leaving anything to chance.' Vicky laughed.

'Not where coffee's concerned. I don't function in the morning until I've had at least two cups.'

'I'll try to remember that,' she replied as she rinsed out the pot and dried it. 'I presume you'd like to try it out now?'

'Can't think of a better time.' He grinned and leaned against the cupboards, watching as she moved around the kitchen.

When she had finished, he took her hand and said, 'Now, show me which room I'm in and where to find things.' He scooped up his bag but didn't let go of her fingers. Vicky realised she was in grave danger where Steven Pearce was concerned—first that devastating kiss, then witnessing his long, muscled legs in tight denim and now having her hand held.

If this was an indication of how the next few days would be, all kissing and touching, then she had no hope whatsoever of surviving unscathed. Steven was becoming like a powerful drug to her system and the cravings were starting to get worse.

She walked ahead of him down the long hallway that connected all the rooms in the old homestead.

'This will be your room.' Vicky opened the door and went in. It was tidy, with only the necessities. Wardrobe, bed, dresser, table lamp.

'Where's your room?' he asked with a hint of a smile.

'D-down at the other end,' she faltered, then blushed as his smile increased.

'Putting distance between us, Vicky?' he asked, one eyebrow raised.

'The bed's more comfortable in here.' She shrugged, before tugging her hand free. 'I'll get you some sheets and towels.' Turning quickly, she almost ran out of the room, down to the laundry where the linen was stored.

Once there, she leaned against the wall, closed her eyes and concentrated on slowing her breathing. It was too dangerous. *He* was too dangerous. Having him this close to her during the most intimate parts of the day, it would be her undoing. She should go out there now and tell him it was a mistake, tell him to stay at the pub for the next few days, but instead she reached out shaking hands to collect the linen and walked, with renewed self-confidence, back to the front end of the house.

That confidence evaporated into thin air when she re-entered the room. There he stood, with his back to her— shirt stripped off, muscled upper torso on display. Her arms went weak, along with her knees, and the bundle she was holding dropped to the floor with a thud. The sound echoed in her mind over and over as her heart pounded out a similar unsteady rhythm.

He turned, then a slow smile spread across his face as he read her reaction. Vicky couldn't help herself. She let her eyes slowly travel over his body. The denim jeans looked even better than before when combined with his naked washboard-like stomach.

Her eyelids closed and she breathed in deeply, trying not to drool. Why, oh, why had he stripped off? Didn't the man have any idea of his sex appeal? His animal magnetism which drew her to him? Of course he did she realised a moment later as she felt his hand touch hers.

'Vicky.' He spoke her name softly as he brought both her hands up and rested her palms against his warm skin.

She opened her eyes. He had a slight smattering of dark hair on his chest but not too much. He was all muscle—not an ounce of fat on him, she realised as her fingers gently moved first downwards, then back up again.

Steven reached out and cupped her face, tilting her head upwards. Vicky looked into his eyes and was once again mesmerised by the brilliant blue colour.

'"What a tangled web we weave,"' he murmured, before lowering his head to claim her lips in a soft and seductive kiss, and she closed her eyes once more.

Vicky parted her lips, accepting the tip of his tongue into her mouth as he playfully tasted and teased. His arms came around her, tenderly running his fingertips up and down her back, and this time Vicky was thankful they didn't have an audience.

She groaned and pressed closer to him as he continued

his onslaught. Steven brought to life emotions she'd never known existed. The knots in her stomach began to unwind as the anxiety of the situation dissolved.

There were only the two of them. Nothing else existed, and as Steven's tongue continued to probe further Vicky felt her self-control evaporate.

Her fingers worked their way to his back and he pulled her closer. With her breasts pressing against his chest, she grew annoyed at the clothing that separated them. As though he had similar thoughts, Steven tugged her shirt from the waistband of her trousers.

His hands, with agonising slowness, ran up her spine, before slipping around to the front. The moment his thumb touched her breast Vicky knew she was lost.

She felt her pulse rate increase as he carefully caressed her, running his fingers around the edge of her lacy bra. Never having felt anything so incredibly sensuous in her life, Vicky's lips broke from his and she gasped for breath.

Steven took the opportunity to trail hot kisses down her neck, before bending his head to continue the rain of fiery kisses around her navel and upwards to where his hands were still cupping her breasts. Her shirt, uncomfortably bunched up under her arms, was of no consequence as his lips pressed against her modest cleavage.

'Steven,' she whispered as her fingers plunged into his hair.

At the sound of his name on her lips, Steven reluctantly stopped his exploration and slowly straightened, pulling her shirt back down. He drew her roughly to him, cradling her head against his chest.

'W-what?' she managed, not at all sure what was happening. One second his lips were causing her body to burn and the next they were gone.

'Shh,' he said. They stood together, Steven holding her close while Vicky allowed her arms to slump beside her.

She listened to his heartbeat as the rhythm began to return to normal.

After a few minutes Steven gave a mirthless laugh, his voice husky as he said, 'Vicky, you make me lose all rational thought.'

'Is…is that good or bad?' Vicky asked softly.

Steven held her from him and looked down into her eyes. 'It's complicated,' he replied seriously.

Vicky searched for something to say that might hopefully lighten the atmosphere but her mind was a complete blank. Such was the effect Steven Pearce had on her system. His gaze was hypnotic, his warm hands still gently caressing her shoulders keeping the fires smouldering within.

'I'm going to take a shower,' he said and for a moment Vicky thought his expression was inviting her to join him. His arms dropped back to his sides and she felt bereft. She looked down at the floor and saw the forgotten linen. Scooping it up, she placed it on the bed and handed Steven a towel.

'Enjoy your shower,' she said, trying to regain her composure. 'I have a clinic this afternoon so I'd better get lunch organised or I'll be consulting on an empty stomach.' Vicky backed to the door.

'Sounds great,' he replied enthusiastically. 'I'm ravenous.'

Vicky should have felt indignant, but the smile he gave her erased all feelings except the emotional mush she was coming to feel whenever around him.

'Right, then.' She nodded firmly, as though clearing the mental fog away and concentrating on the task at hand. Entering the kitchen, she was met with the delicious aroma of freshly percolated coffee. The pot had been a thoughtful gift on his part, even though he'd refused to admit it.

Vicky smiled as she busied herself slicing bread, attempting to get her thoughts into some sort of rational order.

Where Steven Pearce was concerned, she doubted whether that would ever be a possibility—rational thought when the man evoked such wild emotions?

A loud shout came from the direction of the bathroom. Vicky dropped the knife and quickly ran to the door.

'Steven?' she called. 'Are you OK?' Should she go in? she wondered as she waited for a reply. 'Steven?'

The door was wrenched open to display a half-wet man with a blue towel draped low on his hips and an angry red patch down his left arm.

'What's with the water?' he demanded.

'Water?' She hesitated, trying to focus on his words. It was difficult when more than just his torso was on display. The knowledge that, by removing the towel, he was naked underneath was doing worse things to her system than when he'd only been wearing jeans.

'I almost got burned.'

'Sorry,' Vicky replied with sincerity. 'I forgot to mention that it takes a few seconds for the hot water to settle down. It *is* very hot.'

'Now she remembers,' he said with a smile to belie the fierceness of his words.

'Sorry,' she repeated. 'Try turning the cold tap on first and adding a bit of hot water gradually. That's the way I do it.'

'Right.' He shut the door.

Vicky turned slowly, listening in case the hot water attacked again, but when no more shouts came she returned to the kitchen.

Cutting up tomatoes, lettuce and cheese, Vicky tried hard not to think about the naked man in her bathroom. Standing in the same place she stood when she showered. Closing her eyes, she could visualise the water cascading down over his chest before it plunged downwards to—

'Ouch!' Her eyes snapped open as she dropped the knife

and raised her cut finger to her lips. 'Stupid, stupid, stupid.'
She rummaged in the top cupboard for the medicine kit.

Collecting some antiseptic cream and a plaster, she
washed her cut finger, before proceeding to dress it.

'What have you done?' Steven asked, and she turned to
see him walking towards her, pulling a shirt over his head.
The snug-fitting jeans were back in place and his feet were
bare.

'Cut your finger, eh?' he asked when she didn't reply.
'Tut-tut. I should have thought a doctor like yourself would
know better than to let your thoughts wander when there's
a knife in your hand. Good job you didn't decide to become
a surgeon.'

Vicky simply glared at him and returned her attention to
the plaster. Unfortunately, the two ends of the plaster didn't
want to co-operate and stuck themselves together.

'Here.' Steven grasped her hand in his firm grip. 'Let me
help.'

'I'm fine,' Vicky said between clenched teeth, snatching
her hand back. It was all his fault. If he hadn't bulldozed
his way into her home, she would never have been distracted
enough to allow herself to be so careless.

'Now, now, Vicky.' He picked up another plaster, before
once again reaching for her injured finger. 'Any deeper and
it would have needed sutures.'

'Spare me the lectures.'

'Certainly,' he replied. '*Voila!* One bandaged finger. And
now I would like you to pour us both some coffee while I
finish making the sandwiches. After all, we must get you to
the clinic on time.'

Vicky poured coffee for both of them, remembering that
he took it with milk, no sugar, before sitting down at the
table to watch him assemble their lunch. It should seem
strange, having him in her kitchen—her house—but it

didn't. It seemed perfectly natural that Steven felt at home here.

He placed a plate in front of her and said, 'Eat.' It allowed her no further time to dwell on those thoughts.

Realising she was very hungry, Vicky did as she was told.

'You're just like my sister.' Steven shook his head in wonderment. 'She eats like a horse and doesn't seem to put on an ounce of weight. Kath always says that running a department in a busy children's hospital is what keeps the calories off and the appetite up.'

'Sounds like my kind of woman,' Vicky remarked.

'Actually, you and Kath would get along very well. I can already see many similarities. Although I hope you don't have a similar temper.'

'Bad?' Vicky enquired with a smile. When Steven talked about his family, she felt envious at the close relationship they shared. It was the type of relationship she'd wished for with Leesha and Jerome because, although they cared about each other, they had little in common.

'What can I say?' He spread his arms out wide. 'She's a redhead. Poor Jack. I feel sorry for him some days when she really lets fly, but fortunately for him he has a way of defusing it—like that.' Steven snapped his fingers. '*Unfortunately* for the rest of us, we can't employ the same methods.'

Vicky laughed at his meaning. 'I wouldn't say my temper is bad but it does tend to simmer beneath the surface. Unless I'm seriously provoked,' she added.

'Thanks for the warning.'

Vicky glanced at the clock, gasped and bit into another sandwich.

'Problem?' he asked

'Not really. I need to check up on Neil Simpson before my clinic and Friday is usually my busiest afternoon.'

'Start late—finish late.' He nodded. 'I know it all too well. You really enjoy your job, don't you?'

'Love it. I always wanted to practise here and now my dreams have come true.'

'But why do you live so far away from the hospital and your consulting rooms?'

'I'd hardly call a fifteen-minute drive far away, Steven. I'm sure you live farther away from your hospital in the city.'

'I do, but there are always staff there to cover emergencies. Those fifteen minutes you need to drive to the hospital could mean the difference between life and death.'

'Are you suggesting I should live behind the hospital or something?' Vicky's tone held a note of censure.

'Well…it would make more sense. You'd be more accessible to your patients and therefore could give them faster treatment.'

'And what would you suggest I do with this?' Vicky gestured, indicating the room. 'This is my family home. I *love* this place.' The warm, fuzzy feeling she'd been nurturing since Steven had shown up this morning began to dissipate. How dared he criticise her? It was nothing to do with him where she lived.

'You could always sell it,' he suggested.

'What?' Vicky rose to her feet and carried her plate and cup to the sink. 'You've got a lot of nerve, Steven Pearce. Waltzing in here, inviting yourself to stay and then condemning me for living fifteen minutes away from the hospital. If that's your attitude, you can just leave. I don't have to take this kind of abuse in my own home. The *only* home I've ever known.'

She stood before him, her hands planted firmly on her hips. 'You don't seem to have any idea how much I need this place. All my memories are here. My parents brought me here when I was only a few days old and here I'll stay.'

'But it would sell very easily. It's not as though you haven't had offers,' Steven remarked, seemingly unperturbed by her outburst.

'How…?' Vicky gritted her teeth and clenched her hands into fists. She was now spluttering with rage at his audacity. 'How dare you say such things? Do you think because my sister's sold her share of our family property that I automatically want to do the same? Well, I don't. Yes, I've had offers. Nigel Fairweather has made me several and they've all been quite impressive, too.'

'But not enough to induce you to sell.'

'You don't seem to understand. Even if I was offered all the money in the world, I still wouldn't sell. This isn't just land we're talking about. This is my family heritage and you can be assured that as soon as I'm more financially stable I'll be buying the land back. So you can tell your buddy at the Sharlock Wine Company to watch out for Victoria Hansen. It'll be a name he'll never forget.'

With that she stormed out of the room, leaving a stunned Steven sitting at the kitchen table.

There's your answer, Dave, Steven thought, and then winced when Vicky slammed her door. He lifted his coffee-cup to his lips and wondered whether she was serious about him getting out of her house. He hoped not. His best chance of wearing down her defences regarding her beloved house was to be as close to her as possible—for as long as possible.

Not to mention the added bonus of a little flirtation. She was an extremely desirable woman and he definitely wouldn't say no to becoming better acquainted. A lot better acquainted.

The phone rang, interrupting his thoughts. He heard Vicky's door open and the sound of footsteps coming towards the kitchen. The cordless phone was next to him on the table so he picked it up just as she re-entered the kitchen.

'Dr Hansen's residence. Butler speaking.'

Vicky stormed over and held her hand out for the phone. Steven ignored her and mimed writing with his free hand. She spun around, snatched pen and paper off the kitchen bench and slapped it down on the table. Fine. If that was the way he wanted to play it, *he* could deal with the call.

Returning to her room, she brushed her hair with more aggression than was necessary, such was her frustration at Steven's high-handedness. Placing the brush back on the dresser, she forced herself to take three slow and steady breaths. That done, she applied her lipstick, checked that her shirt and trousers were still clean and pronounced herself ready for work.

Vicky wasn't sure whether she really wanted Steven to leave or not. Part of her did, but as for the rest… Her body *definitely* wanted him to stay.

Annoyed at her indecision, she made her way back to the kitchen to find Steven sitting down, frantically scribbling notes, a deep frown creasing his forehead.

'How long until the ambulance arrives, Nicole?' he asked briskly, and noted the information. There was another pause, then he said, 'No. I'll need her with me. Can you arrange for this afternoon's clinic and home visit to Neil Simpson to be rescheduled? Good. We'll be there soon.' With that he hung up.

Vicky hadn't moved from the doorway. The fact that Steven Pearce seemed to be rearranging her life had nothing to do with the apprehension rippling through her.

'Who is it?' she asked quietly, all animosity towards him forgotten in the light of a medical emergency.

'Fred Durrant. He's had a bad car accident. Drove into a tree. He's alive but badly injured according to the preliminary report the hospital has received. Nicole said that Daniel and Mac should reach him within minutes so it would probably be another half-hour at least before they return to the hospital.'

'Daniel's our police officer,' Vicky told him, not knowing whether he knew it or not. 'Where did it happen?'

'On the last bend before his farm.'

Vicky nodded. 'At least that's not too far out of town.' She took a breath, pushing away the shock and drawing on the strength she needed. 'I heard you say you'd need my help.'

'I'll need you in Theatre with me.' He stood. 'Get your things and let's get to the hospital, stat.' He walked past her and disappeared into his room. Seconds later he was back and ready to leave.

'We'll take my car,' he said as he went out the back door.

Not wanting to argue the point, Vicky followed. Steven seemed to be deep in thought on the drive to the hospital and she didn't want to disturb him. Car accidents usually involved bad orthopaedic trauma injuries and she knew his mind was working overtime, trying to visualise different scenarios.

The hospital was peaceful—at least on the surface. When they walked down the corridor that lead to the theatres, the atmosphere changed to one of grim anticipation. That's where they found Nicole.

'What's the latest?' Steven asked. 'Do we have a list of his injuries yet?'

Nicole handed him a chart. 'Just came in from Daniel. He radioed it through and said that Mac should be here within ten minutes.'

Steven read the list out loud. 'Cuts and abrasions to face, query skull fracture, neck secured with brace, fractured left and right ulnas, fractured right femur, query right neck of femur, bruising to right ribs from steering-wheel.'

He shook his head at the list. 'How old is Fred?'

'Ninety-seven,' Vicky answered. Their eyes locked and

both realised the danger. Although none of the injuries Steven had read out were life-threatening individually, in combination, under these circumstances, and with Fred's age, they were.

'I sincerely hope he's in good health.'

Vicky nodded. 'Exercises frequently, is a non smoker and has a few beers once a week at the pub with his mates.'

Steven acknowledged the information, before turning to Nicole. 'I'm presuming he's stabilised?'

'Yes, Doctor. Mac has reported pulse, blood pressure and neurological observations as stable.'

'The instant that ambulance pulls up, I'll examine him. Then I need X-rays of everything, stat. Give me the forms and I'll fill them out.'

'The forms can wait until later, Mr Pearce,' Nicole informed him with a small smile, indicating that a smaller hospital didn't necessarily run with the same protocols as the larger teaching hospitals he was used to. 'Tell me what you need and I'll arrange it.'

'Skull X-ray, both arms and hands, right femur and vertebral column.' Steven paused and checked the chart again. 'You've noted he's already had total hip replacements on both sides so do a pelvic X-ray to check them, although, considering Mac has queried the neck of the femur, I'll probably need to replace the prosthesis but that can wait until later. Do we know his blood type?'

Nicole quickly scanned Fred's case notes, before saying, 'O-positive.'

'Have two units ready to go. Vicky.' He turned to her. 'You'll be assisting me.'

She gave him a nod. It seemed a decade ago that she'd done her orthopaedic rotation but she was sure Steven would tell her what he needed and when.

'Who's the anaesthetist?'

'I am,' Emma said from the doorway. She smiled at

Vicky and Nicole, before extending her hand in welcome to Steven. 'Emma Travis. I'm sorry to be meeting you under such circumstances as these.'

Steven shook her hand. 'So am I.'

'We just thank God you're here, Doctor,' Nicole said, and everyone agreed.

If Steven hadn't come down until Sunday evening—his job not officially beginning until Monday—then Fred would have been stabilised as much as possible then airlifted to Adelaide. Vicky was unsure whether he would have survived the extra trauma but thankfully that was one scenario they didn't need to worry about.

As the minutes ticked by Steven gave orders left, right and centre. The new orthopaedic surgeon was in charge and everyone was bowing to his expertise. 'Do you have a general surgeon on your staff?' he asked Vicky.

'Yes, but he's on leave for six months. I've done courses in general surgery and basic trauma care, though, as it's necessary for a country GP to have up-to-date qualifications, so we'll handle the situation.'

'I'm sure we will,' Steven replied with a confident smile. 'So you hold a diploma in general surgery? You are full of surprises.'

'Thank you.' She glanced around at the team of professionals waiting for their patient. 'Looks as though we're well organised here.'

'Yes. Now all we need—' Steven broke off as the wail of the siren could be heard drawing closer. 'Finally,' he said, and walked briskly out to meet the ambulance.

CHAPTER SIX

MAC had done his job well in stabilising Fred. Analgesics had been given at the accident site so their patient wasn't in too much pain and an oxygen mask was over his nose and mouth.

'He's been lapsing in and out of consciousness,' Mac reported to Steven, 'but thankfully the blood loss has been minimal.'

'Right,' Steven said once he'd examined Fred and was satisfied. 'Let's get those X-rays done. Is Dorothy here somewhere?'

'Yes, Doctor,' Nicole said. 'Faith drove her here not long after the ambulance arrived. She's in my office.'

'I'll go speak to her.' He looked at Vicky. 'Would you mind accompanying me? I'm sure Dorothy would appreciate it.'

'Certainly.' Vicky nodded.

He was at the door when he turned back to Nicole. He opened his mouth to speak but Nicole said, 'I'll contact you the instant the films are done, Doctor.'

Steven gave her a smile. 'Thank you, Sister.' He strode off, leaving Vicky to follow in his wake.

Faith had stayed with Dorothy as they'd sat in Nicole's office. The desk was, predictably, neat and tidy. The room might have been called sterile-looking if it hadn't been for the beautiful vase of fresh daffodils that sat on the window-sill. Two mugs of tea sat untouched on the small table beside the two women who were anxiously awaiting news.

'Dorothy.' Steven placed his hand reassuringly on her shoulder.

The elderly woman looked up at him with red-rimmed eyes. 'Oh, Dr Pearce,' Dorothy sobbed. 'Is he going to be all right?'

Steven pulled up chairs for himself and Vicky, and spoke calmly, choosing his words with care. 'Fred is coping reasonably well with the shock and trauma his body is going through. At the moment, he's having X-rays taken so I can determine exactly what needs to be done.'

'We're so grateful you're here, Steven,' Faith chimed in as she continued to clutch Dorothy's hands in hers.

'Yes, yes,' said Dorothy, nodding. She took a deep breath before saying, 'What's going to happen?'

'From Mac's report and my initial examination, we will need to operate within the next few hours. Fred has fractured his right femur—that's the thigh bone—and I'll need to fix that back together with a long metal rod. It's a straightforward procedure that will require him to have the rod removed in about two years' time.'

Vicky watched the shadow of doubt cross Dorothy's face and knew what was coming.

'But he's ninety-seven now. What if…what if…?' Dorothy stopped, unable to complete her sentence. She had no need, as everyone in the room knew what was on her mind.

'I don't think you'll have too much to worry about, Dorothy.' Vicky smiled. 'Both of Fred's parents lived until they were one hundred and eight so my guess is he'll be around for quite a few more years. He'll still be at the pub on a Friday night with the men, he'll still be snoring and keeping you awake nearly every night and he'll still be leaving his dirty socks on the floor.'

This brought a small smile to Dorothy's sad face. 'I don't think I'll *ever* be able to get him to pick up his socks.'

'You're probably right there,' Steven agreed. And I can tell you he *definitely* won't be picking up much in the near future. He has two broken arms but thankfully they look like nice, clean breaks so a simple plaster cast on each arm should do the trick. They'll be from the wrist to the elbow so he'll still be able to wiggle his fingers around. The casts will need to be on for two or three months and then— *voila*—two fixed bones.

'Apart from that, he has a mild concussion which will mean severe headaches, but these can be controlled with analgesics. The only other fly in the ointment is his right hip. I know he had a hip replacement done a few years back and he appears to have dislocated the prosthesis. I'll know more when I see the X-rays but I won't be doing anything about that today. Fred has enough to cope with and he won't be walking around for the next few days so we have a bit of time up our sleeves.'

'How long will he be in hospital?' Dorothy asked.

'Between two and four weeks. As I said, it all depends on what the X-rays show regarding his hip.'

There was a knock at the door then Nicole opened it. 'The first set of X-rays are ready for review, Doctor.'

'Thank you.' Steven rose to his feet. 'Dorothy, I'll be back later to let you know what's happening. We don't want you to feel left out in any way. If you have any questions ask either Vicky or myself, and if we're not around write them down.'

'How long will the operation take?'

'About an hour once we get into Theatre. As I said, I'll come back and talk to you after I've reviewed all the X-rays. That probably won't be for another thirty to forty minutes, so I'll see you then.'

Steven went with Nicole but Vicky stayed. 'Dorothy, you know you're more than welcome to sleep at the hospital tonight—in fact, I think it will do Fred more good if you're beside him. That means you'll be needing a change of clothes and so will Fred. If you don't feel comfortable leaving the hospital, perhaps Faith can arrange for someone to do it for you. Either way, when Fred comes around from the anaesthetic he'll be needing you.'

Dorothy blew her nose. 'I know I have to be strong for him. It's just so…hard.'

'I know,' Vicky said, reaching out a hand to her. She knew the only way to help Dorothy was to help Fred. This was the reason she'd become a doctor. To do her best to heal people and get them on the road to recovery. 'I need to go now and see if there's anything I can do to help Steven.' Vicky's eyes met those of Faith who nodded reassuringly.

'Faith will be here with you and I'm sure most of the town knows about the accident and will be there to support you both.'

'Off you go, dear,' Dorothy said. 'Give Fred my love.'

'I will,' she promised, before leaving the room.

Walking through the small X-ray department, which was located near the front of the hospital, she knew she'd find Steven in the viewing room. Although they were a country hospital, their machinery and equipment was quite modern.

'What's the news?' she asked as he peered at the X-rays of Fred's spinal column.

'Everything here looks fine.' He pointed to another X-ray of the pelvis. 'The right total hip prosthesis has been dislocated, as you can see here.' Because the prosthesis was made of metal, it appeared white and very defined on the black and white X-rays whereas bone appeared a dense grey colour. 'As you can see, the prosthesis has been bent so I'll need a new one to replace it. If it had simply slipped out, I would have been able to relocate it quite easily.'

'When will you operate on it?'

'Depending on how Fred copes with today's theatre session, probably in a week. In this situation, I have around seven to ten days before it becomes a necessity.'

'Let me know if you need any help.' Vicky's voice broke on the last word as she met Steven's gaze.

They were silent for a moment. It was the first time they'd been alone since arriving at the hospital. His blue eyes were so intense and so communicative that Vicky felt that all too familiar pull toward him. Her throat went dry and her knees began to wobble.

'Vic...' he murmured, and reached out a hand to her.

It dropped instantly back to his side as the door opened and Nicole came in to deliver the next set of X-rays.

Vicky looked to the floor, cross with herself for being hypnotised once again by Steven's gaze. How did he manage to wipe all thought from her mind—especially when she was still simmering with annoyance at his careless comments regarding her family land?

She quickly schooled her feelings and slipped back into professional mode. Steven hooked the X-rays onto a viewing box and all three of them had a close look at the radiographs of Fred's skull.

'These look fine,' Steven said with satisfaction. 'Nicole, I need to do a total hip replacement for Fred. Probably not until next week, so would you order a hip prosthesis for him? Same brand, type and measurements as before. It obviously works for Fred, so let's not change things.'

'Certainly, Doctor,' Nicole replied. 'These are the final set of X-rays so, if you'll excuse me, I have some paperwork to get organised.'

After Nicole had left, Vicky picked up the X-rays of Fred's arm and had a closer look.

'The fractures to his arms don't look too bad.'

'As I suspected,' Steven replied, his eyes still scanning the skull X-rays. 'Simple fractures that we can fix with plaster casts.' He pulled the films off the viewing box and gathered them up.

'We'll begin in Theatre within the hour.' He looked at

the clock—almost half past two. 'I'd like to focus on nailing the femur first. We'll have to be careful of that dislocated hip but it shouldn't be too much of a problem. Once that's done, Emma can reverse the anaesthetic and we'll apply the plaster casts. At his age, I don't want him anaesthetised for too long.'

'I must admit, Steven,' Vicky said anxiously, 'I haven't done orthopaedics for quite some time, but as long as you're specific I'm sure I'll get through.'

He gave her his winning smile and her insides instantly turned to mush.

'I intend to be—and not just in the operating theatre.' Before she could reply he said, 'Come, Dr Hansen. Let's get Fred organised.'

Once they'd scrubbed and gowned, Steven and Vicky entered the theatre, where Emma was at the head of their anaesthetised patient, monitoring the dials closely.

'I realise it's been a while,' Steven addressed the theatre staff, 'since most of you have done any orthopaedic assisting. Considering we've never worked together as a team, there may be some tension as you learn my techniques and methods.' He looked around the room.

'I will tell you now that I don't tolerate incompetence in my theatre. As theatre staff we are all experienced in our fields, but as a team we're only at the beginning. Therefore, if anyone has questions—for example, which retractor to pass me or when to suction, and so on—please, ask. I am more than willing to guide and help you to know what I need done. Please, do not just jump in and do what you think might be the right thing. If it feels as though you're asking questions during the entire operation, that's fine with me.

'After consultation with Emma, we feel it's best not to have Fred anaesthetised for too long, so, without further lecturing from your new surgeon, I suggest we begin.' His blue eyes met Vicky's and he gave her a brisk nod. He was a doctor first and foremost and his entire attention was focused on his patient.

She was grateful for his spiel as the atmosphere when they'd walked into Theatre had been one of apprehension and unease. Now they all had direction and their leader was more than willing to help and discuss, to guide the team in unison.

'The procedure we'll be performing today is fixing Fred's fractured right femur with a metal rod. This will be inserted down the cavity of the bone and then nailed into place. After incision I need to debride the wound, then the nailing procedure can begin. I'll need a check X-ray before I close in layers, which will be number one Vicryl, double zero Vicryl and then staples. Thankfully, there has been minimal blood loss and the fractures to his arms can be secured with plaster casts.

'Once I've completed the rodding technique and closed, Emma will reverse the anaesthetic. The casts will be applied after this. Sounds nice and simple so, without further ado, let's get down to business.'

And that's exactly what they did. Steven was an extremely competent surgeon who gave clear and concise instructions. There were one or two minor questions from other staff, but for the most part the new orthopaedic theatre team was functioning like a well-oiled piece of machinery.

Vicky's initial apprehension was unnecessary as she found herself pre-empting Steven's need for her assistance. Perhaps she hadn't forgotten as much as she'd thought.

When the operation was over, Emma reversed the anaesthetic and pronounced herself extremely happy with Fred's stabilisation.

'Plaster casts are next,' Steven announced as he and Vicky pulled off their gloves and degowned. The plaster mix was ready, as were the bandages, for their attention.

Vicky once again assisted him and their teamwork became stronger.

He was now a very integral part of the McLoughlin Vale Hospital and Vicky knew he would come to care for the people of this community the way she and the other medical staff did. None of the staff would leave tonight until they were each satisfied with Fred's progress and had spoken to Dorothy, offering their help in any way they could.

When the casts were in place Fred was wheeled to Recovery where the nursing staff would monitor him very closely. Considering he was their only patient, he was bound to get undivided attention.

After she and Steven had removed their protective garments and washed their hands again, Vicky stood back and watched him yawn and stretch, raising his arms above his head.

'What I wouldn't give for a long, cool, glass of beer.' He grinned.

'Beer?' she asked with interest. 'I thought most surgeons wanted tea or coffee or even a massage after Theatre—but beer?'

He lowered his arms and gave her an inviting look. 'If you're *offering* a massage, who am I to refuse?'

Vicky could feel herself growing hot at his suggestion. She cleared her throat, 'Well…I wasn't…exactly offering to—'

'Vicky,' he interrupted, 'I was just teasing. Why don't you go to the tearoom and relax? I need to go and see Dorothy.' That said, he turned on his heel and left.

Vicky stood for a moment, watching until he'd disappeared around a corner. 'A beer,' she mumbled. 'Typical! The man is anything but predictable, you should realise that by now, Vic,' she told herself as she made her way to the female change rooms.

Getting out of her theatre garb and back into her trousers

and shirt, Vicky went to check on Fred. The recovery nurses were happy with his progress, and once Vicky had quickly looked at his notes she left them to their work.

'Beer,' she mumbled again, and shook her head.

'Pardon?' Nicole asked from behind her. Vicky turned around to grin at her friend.

'I said, "beer".'

'That's what I thought, but you don't drink beer.'

'No, but Steven Pearce does. He told me that he likes a coldie after operations.'

'Why, then, are you walking around mumbling about beer?'

Vicky looked at the floor and then back to Nicole again. 'Well, I was thinking about asking him to come to the pub when he's finished. After all, he is new in town and might not know where the pub is.'

'What's stopping you?' Nicole asked, trying not to smile.

'You know how crowded it is at this time of day—especially on a Friday.'

'I do. The men finish their work early and start the drinking early. Friday's are always worse than any other night of the week for occurrence of minor injuries,' Nicole said. 'Are you trying to tell me you're not sure whether you want the community to see you and Steven enjoying a drink at the pub after a hard day's work?'

'Well...' Vicky hesitated.

'Because you're entitled to drink there just like everyone else. Besides,' Nicole said, allowing her smile to brighten her face, 'people will know soon enough that the man is living with you.'

Vicky's jaw dropped. 'How do...?'

'He told me. I need to know where to find my medical staff.'

'It's not what you think,' Vicky protested, and Nicole placed her hand on Vicky's shoulder.

'I'm not thinking anything and it shouldn't matter what anyone else says or thinks either. If you like this man then go for it. You deserve some happiness.'

'Yes,' Vicky agreed slowly, 'but is Steven Pearce the man to give it to me?' Her thoughts wandered back to their previous conversation regarding her family land. As she remembered it, the annoyance and frustration at his lack of understanding returned.

'Now there's a loaded question.' Nicole laughed. 'Start with a drink and go from there. It's not as though you'd be alone,' she pointed out.

'True. Thanks.' Vicky turned around but wasn't sure where she might find Steven.

'He's getting changed,' Nicole informed her.

'Thanks again.' Vicky nodded and headed for the male change rooms. She waited outside, trying her hardest not to remember the way he looked stripped to the waist. Or the feel of his skin beneath her fingertips. Or the scent of his cologne after he'd showered.

She leaned back against the wall and closed her eyes. Giving in to her memories, Vicky licked her lips, recalling all too easily the taste of his kisses.

'Where are you and may I join you?' a deep voice whispered in her ear.

Vicky sprang away from the wall, her eyes snapping open in horror at being discovered.

'Ste-Steven,' she stammered.

He raised an eyebrow at her, a knowing smile on his face. 'Were you expecting someone else?'

'Uh… No.'

'Then you were waiting for me,' he stated.

'Yes.' Come on, Vicky, she told herself. You have an intelligent mind, surely you can do better than monosyllables.

'So what can I do for you?'

'Pub,' she replied, and groaned at her inability to form a coherent sentence. Closing her eyes, she took a deep breath and then looked at him.

'I was waiting to ask you to join me for that coldie at the pub.'

'Great idea. I'll check on Fred and then we can go.' They walked down the corridor to Recovery. Dorothy and Faith were at Fred's bedside when they arrived. Steven read the chart, chatted to Dorothy and roused Fred for a few moments' consciousness, before allowing him to continue sleeping off the effects of the general anaesthetic.

He gave the nurses orders and signed for the required doses of analgesics. After discussion with Emma, and making a few more notes on Fred's chart, he turned to Vicky and said, 'Let's go have that drink.'

'Oh, are you going to the pub?' Faith asked, and collected her handbag off the chair. 'Mind if we come, too?'

'Not at all,' Vicky answered a little too quickly.

'I know Fred's in the best of care,' Dorothy said with a smile. 'And I'd like to tell all his mates at the pub that he's just fine.'

'Then what are we waiting for?' Steven held out his arm to Dorothy.

The four of them took their time walking the short distance to the old sandstone building which had held many a party. As soon as Dorothy stepped through the door, a cheer went up and beer glasses were raised high in a salute to her husband.

'Pipe down,' John, the proprietor, who was serving behind the counter, ordered. When the place was quiet he said, 'Well, Doc?' And looked to Steven for the answer.

'Fred is stabilised and doing fine. He needs another operation, but apart from that he's out of danger.'

'That's what we wanted to hear,' John replied. 'Come and sit down at the bar and have a drink. On me.'

'Thank you,' Steven said. Faith and Dorothy went to talk to some friends sitting at a table so Steven escorted Vicky to a bar stool. She felt as though everyone's eyes were on them, but when she casually glanced around the room she found she was wrong. No one seemed to care she was here with the handsome new doctor and that was because they'd already labelled them an item.

So sit back, relax and enjoy it, she told herself. She drank two glasses of soft drink while Steven slowly drank his beer.

'Would you like another one?' she asked, and he shook his head.

'I only ever have one. No more and even then always a light beer.'

'There's a story there,' she guessed, and he nodded.

'Almost wrecked my career when I was an intern. It changed my entire attitude to drinking and I've never found it pleasurable to get drunk since.'

'That's *all* you're going to tell me? There must be a woman involved somewhere?' she teased.

Steven laughed. 'How did you know? I'd just finished an all-nighter in Theatre when I met up with some friends from the vascular department—or, should I say, the petite blonde vascular registrar I'd been wooing asked me along. They'd just finished the night shift as well and were going to the pub for breakfast.'

'Interesting. The *pub* for breakfast?'

'Are you going to interrupt throughout this entire story?' he chided.

'Sorry.' Vicky placed a finger over her lips, indicating she'd remain quiet.

'One of the guys was getting married so we all started celebrating. I was exhausted and had hardly eaten a thing so the alcohol went straight to my head. Everything would have been all right if I hadn't forgotten to collect my textbooks before I left the hospital.'

'You were caught drunk in hospital grounds.'

'I was caught by the *professor* drunk in the hospital grounds. I would have failed my rotation, if not the entire year, and been punished with disciplinary action. As it turned out, my sister intervened for me and I only had a permanent account of it on my record. No further action was deemed necessary.'

'Good to have a sister with connections, eh?'

'Connections? She ended up marrying the professor.' Steven grinned. 'Yeah. I really owed Kath one for that. I guess it was her disappointment in me that really clinched it for me. I didn't drink alcohol again until I'd passed my final orthopaedic exams and was officially a surgeon. Even then, it was tempered to just a few drinks.'

'And the vascular registrar?' Vicky asked, trying not to feel slightly jealous of any other woman who had held Steven's interest.

'The who?' he asked, squinting as though trying to recall the woman.

'I see.' Vicky laughed, glad that nothing had come of his infatuation.

'So there you have it. A small delve into the psyche of Steven Pearce.'

'Very small but worth listening to all the same.' Vicky smiled. 'Thank you.'

During the hour they were there everyone in the room stopped to say a few words of thanks to them, and Vicky's heart felt renewed with the caring attitude of the community.

At half past five she glanced at her watch and groaned.

'What's the matter?' Steven asked.

'I need to see Neil Simpson. His mother will be getting dinner ready and then the bedtime routine will begin. I don't want to disrupt the family any more than I have.'

'You'd better go, then. Here.' He reached into his pocket and pulled out his keys. 'Take my car.'

'I have to stop and see Mary as well,' she confessed, but took the keys.

He shrugged. 'No problem. I'll get a lift home.'

Not knowing whether she was happy with this or not, Vicky nodded.

'See you, then,' Steven said, and leaned in to kiss her softly on the lips.

The conversations around them came to a halt and Vicky wished the ground would open up and swallow her.

'You've just sealed your fate,' she whispered shakily to Steven as she gripped the keys tightly.

'Wrong.' He raised one eyebrow. 'I've just sealed *our* fates.'

CHAPTER SEVEN

VICKY pushed all thoughts of Steven out of her mind, which was easier said than done. She stopped at the hospital and quickly collected the black medical bag she kept fully stocked in her office and then called on Neil.

His mother reported no unusual symptoms, other than driving her around the twist. 'He's a real terror.' She ruffled his hair affectionately. 'Always has been and always will be.' The love for her son as she said these words was clearly visible in her eyes.

Vicky laughed as she repacked her bag, after giving Neil a check-up. 'You can get out and about tomorrow, but don't overdo it,' she cautioned him.

'No, Dr Hansen,' he promised eagerly. 'I've been trying my best to do what Mum says and I've done all my school work.'

'Good boy.' Vicky nodded and stood up. 'I have to get going but I'd like to see Neil in my clinic at the end of next week.'

'I'll make an appointment,' said Mrs Simpson.

Vicky said goodbye to Neil and the rest of his family, before climbing into Steven's car. It was a pleasure to drive, and had she been able to afford such a luxury she'd have bought a new car a long time ago. For the moment her current car did the job nicely, so she didn't complain.

Glancing at the clock on the dashboard, Vicky decided to drop in and see how Mary was doing. She'd detected no signs of postnatal depression during the week, and although a few days had passed since she'd seen her friend they had spoken on the phone every day.

After pulling up in the driveway, she collected her bag and walked to the back door. Giving two short knocks, Vicky walked in, calling a greeting as she went.

'Hi,' Jeff said as he stood in the kitchen, stirring a pot on the stove. 'You're just in time for dinner.'

'Thanks, but I can't stay. I just wanted to check up on Mary. How are you both coping?'

'Mary's cried a few times this week but on the whole she hasn't been over-emotional,' Jeff replied. 'To all intents and purposes, she's handling the loss very well. I'm proud of her.'

'You'll let me know if anything out of the ordinary happens?'

'I'll be on the phone before you know it,' he promised.

'And how about you? How are you coping?'

Jeff shrugged his shoulders. 'Naturally, I'm upset about Stuart but I really feel for Mary. I guess it's different for men. We don't have that immediate bond with our unborn child that the mother has. I hadn't even felt the little tacker kick, but Mary had. We talk about him openly, especially with the children, as we believe it's the best way to grieve.'

'It is. Ah, here she is,' Vicky said as Mary came into the kitchen. The two friends embraced.

'And to what do we owe this visit?' Mary asked.

'A house call. Off to the bedroom so I can give you a check-up.'

'Vicky…' Mary protested.

'Oh, shush,' Vicky ordered. 'Come on, let's get it over and done with before Jeff's finished cooking dinner.'

Mary sat on her bed while Vicky pulled her portable sphygmomanometer out and checked her blood pressure.

'Good.' Vicky nodded when she was finished. 'Normal. Lie back on the bed, please.'

Mary did as she was asked.

'Pop this under your tongue…' she placed a thermometer in her friend's mouth '…while I check the fundus.'

'What's the fundus again?' Mary asked out of the side of her mouth.

Vicky shook her head and tut-tutted. 'I've explained this to you before but I'll be patient and explain it again. It's the inner surface of the dome of the womb. If I press gently on your stomach…' Vicky did so '…I can feel if the size has decreased from the last time I checked, which in this instance it has. If it was still swollen that would indicate infection, and at the moment that's the last thing you need. I'm happy to say everything appears normal. Any fluid retention? Swelling around your fingers?'

Mary shook her head and Vicky nodded again.

'Good. Your pulse is next and then we're finished.' She picked up Mary's wrist and counted the beats. 'Excellent,' she announced, and reached for the thermometer. 'Thirty-six degrees Celsius—normal.'

'May I sit up now?' Mary asked as Vicky began packing her things back into her bag.

'Yes. The medical interrogation is over.'

'And now your interrogation begins.' Mary's eyes sparkled with excitement. 'So…how is he?'

'Who? Steven?' Vicky asked offhandedly, and Mary chuckled.

'He's got you in a spin, hasn't he? Good. It's about time someone did.'

'It's just so frustrating.' Vicky shut her bag with more force than was necessary. 'I'm so attracted to the man and the worst thing is *he* knows it.'

'Why is that bad? Obviously he's attracted to you.'

'Yeah, I guess so.' Vicky sat down on the bed and tried to get her thoughts into some sort of order. Mary, as usual, waited patiently.

'I enjoy being with him, we share the same sense of humour.' Vicky closed her eyes, remembering. 'I melt whenever he touches me and his kisses...his kisses are so passionate and mind-numbing.' She opened her eyes and looked at her friend. 'I've never felt this way about any man before. *Never!*'

'So what's the problem?'

'He's also the most stubborn, opinionated, arrogant and frustrating man I've ever met.'

Mary raised her eyebrows with interest. 'That sounds promising.'

Vicky shook her head. 'He's bullied his way into my house and then keeps picking fights with me.'

'Wait.' Mary held up a hand. 'Steven Pearce is *living* with you?'

'Yes. See what I mean?'

'Not in the slightest. Why don't you start from the beginning?'

'He's staying in the cottage on Leesha's land, and because the plumbing's not done yet he's decided that my house is a suitable alternative. Just announced he was staying.'

'You could have said no,' Mary countered.

'No, I couldn't have.' She looked her friend in the eyes and said slowly, 'I *want* him to stay. I *like* him being near me...but then he'll do something completely arrogant and I just want to throttle him.'

'As I said, it sounds promising.'

Vicky's temper flared. 'Will you stop saying that and tell me what I'm supposed to do?'

'All right, all right.' Mary laughed. 'Calm down. Let me summarise. Steven makes you boiling hot both mentally and emotionally.'

'No...yes,' Vicky admitted.

'You like having him around and you love it when he's passionate.'

Vicky felt butterflies in her stomach at the mere thought of his passionate kisses and smiled shyly. 'Yes,' she answered softly.

'Then I'd say you're hooked.'

'Hooked?'

'In love.'

'I am not.' Vicky quickly refuted Mary's comment. 'I hardly know the man.'

'When it's right, it's right.' Mary shrugged nonchalantly.

'I am not in love with Steven Pearce,' Vicky said emphatically. 'The man... Do you *know* what he said to me?'

'No, but I'm sure you're going to tell me.'

'He had the gall to accuse me of not being a good doctor because I live too far away from the hospital should an emergency come in.'

Mary frowned. 'But you're less than fifteen minutes away. Where are you supposed to live?'

'Well, according to the great Mr Pearce, I'm supposed to live beside the hospital or at my clinic rooms.'

'Dr Loveday used to live farther out than you do and there was never a problem with that.'

'Exactly. He made me so mad...' Vicky clenched her hands into fists and gritted her teeth. 'He barges his way into my home and then calmly announces how I should run my life.'

Mary was thoughtful for a moment and then said, 'Perhaps he's thinking along different lines.'

'What do you mean?'

'Maybe our new orthopaedic surgeon is planning on staying permanently in this area—you know, looking to settle down. Get married and start a family.'

'Steven?'

'You know him better than I do,' Mary replied. 'He could be sounding you out to see how you feel about moving closer into town. How you feel about marriage and children.'

'No.' Vicky shook her head. 'Steven is definitely not husband material. He's more interested in an affair to remember. While he's starting his clinics down south, he's amusing himself with me.'

'If that is true, do you mind?'

'Of course I mind. As you said on Sunday, I *want* to get married and have a family, but Steven Pearce is not a potential husband.'

'Why not? How do you know?'

'It's his type. I'll bet he has a string of broken-hearted women a mile long behind him, and I'm not going to be one of them.'

'Sounds as though you're too late. You're smitten with him.'

'You've seen too many romantic movies.'

'Be honest with yourself,' Mary implored. 'Look at *your* track record. How many broken hearts have you left behind you?'

'Huh. I doubt if *any* of them were broken. Perhaps their egos were a little bent out of shape, but hearts? Broken? Not those guys.'

'Don't be too sure. What about Craig?'

'Craig? Nope. Definitely his ego that was bruised.'

'But it was starting to get serious between the two of you. You even brought him home to meet your mother. That was a big step for you.'

'Actually, it was his idea. He hounded at me until I said yes.'

'See?' Mary threw out her arms. 'When a man starts getting a little bit more serious than you like, you push him away.'

'I was trying to graduate from medical school. Craig simply didn't understand my commitment.'

'But Steven does,' Mary said softly. 'Besides, you've graduated, you've moved back home and bought the practice—everything you've been working towards has happened. You can't use those excuses any more, Vicky. Are you sure you're not trying to create new ones by insisting that Steven *isn't* husband material?'

Vicky sighed and stood. 'Just because we're attracted to each other, it doesn't mean he's the one.' She began to pace the room. 'Sure I like spending time with him. What woman wouldn't? He's a very handsome and appealing man. Just so long as I keep a hold of my emotions—'

'Can you do that?' Mary asked, and Vicky ignored her.

'And don't let things go too far—'

'But if you say stop, will he?' Mary interrupted again.

Vicky thought for a moment, before saying. 'He already has.'

Mary waited and Vicky expounded. 'I walked into his room with towels and sheets and things and there he was, stripped to the waist, wearing only snug-fitting denim jeans.' Her eyes took on a glazed look as she recalled the details.

'We started kissing and when I was ready to throw myself at him he pulled away. When I asked him why he told me things were too complicated.'

'See!' Mary smiled triumphantly. 'He does have plans.'

The glazed look disappeared and Vicky laughed at her friend. 'You have a one-track mind, Mary Jamieson, but you are right about one thing.'

'What?'

'I'm kidding myself about saying no to him because when the moment comes I'll be saying yes, yes, yes.'

They were both silent, absorbing their conversation. Finally, Mary said, 'There comes a time in your life when you need to take some chances. Is this one of them? If you know Steven is offering an affair, are you prepared to settle for that? Or do you put as much distance between the two of you as possible and hold out for that husband you're after? The one who will settle down and help fill that big empty house with the sound of children's laughter?'

'I don't know,' Vicky whispered. 'I'm even more confused now than before.'

There was a knock at the door and Jeff opened it. 'Are you finished yet? Dinner's ready and the kids are starting to crawl up the walls with hunger.'

'Coming, darling.' Mary smiled and stood up. 'Are you staying to eat with us?'

'Not tonight. I have a house guest to attend to.'

'Good luck,' Mary whispered as the friends hugged before Vicky walked out to Steven's car.

As she let herself into her house, the grandfather clock chimed eight o'clock. The smell of steak and garlic welcomed her, and she walked into the kitchen to find Steven busy at the stove.

'Hi,' she said, and he turned to smile at her. Vicky felt her knees begin to collapse and quickly sat down on a stool under the bench. He seemed even more handsome than a few hours ago, and with her recent conversation with Mary still uppermost in her mind Vicky felt her breathing turn shallow with anticipation.

'I wasn't sure what time you'd be back so I decided to start on dinner.'

'Thanks.' Vicky watched in silence as he checked the steaks and stirred a pot. Was Mary right? Did Steven have something more permanent in mind for the two of them?

'Who said you could sit down?' He pointed to the fridge. 'Make the salad and cut the bread.'

Vicky smiled and did as she was asked. Perhaps the next time he made any comments about her property she should answer differently to gauge his reaction. If he was suggesting a more permanent relationship, the last thing she wanted to do was push him away. Although he'd given the impression of being a confirmed bachelor, Vicky was happy to be proved wrong in her estimation of his character. When he'd kissed her at the pub, he'd said he'd sealed *their* fates. Did that mean—?

'Make sure you concentrate this time to avoid cutting your finger,' Steven whispered in her ear.

He startled her so much that she almost jumped out of her skin. The knife slipped from her fingers and clattered onto the bench.

'Hey.' He placed a hand on her shoulder and turned her to face him. 'I was only joking. Are you all right?'

'Y-yes,' Vicky stammered, and raised her eyes to meet his. She felt so foolish.

'You were miles away,' he said, then narrowed his gaze. 'Is everything all right with Mary? Neil Simpson?'

'Yes. They're both fine.' Being so close to him, it was making her lose her perspective. Every word he now said she was trying to decipher, trying to find a hidden meaning. 'I...excuse me,' she mumbled, and swivelled out of his grasp, before running from the kitchen to her bedroom.

Leaning against the closed door, Vicky buried her face in her hands, embarrassment washing over her. Taking deep breaths, she lowered her hands and quickly changed out of her work clothes into jeans and T-shirt.

'You're being ridiculous,' she chided herself as she raked a comb through her hair. 'Forget your conversation with Mary and get a hold on yourself, regardless of whatever hidden meanings may or may not be behind his words...' She jabbed a finger at her reflection. 'Forget them. Just enjoy being with him. Appreciating the time and effort he's put into preparing this meal.'

Giving herself a forceful nod, she pasted on a smile and opened her door, only to find a masculine shirt-covered chest in her way. Steven's hand was raised to knock. She looked up and the smile slid from her face. He was extraordinarily handsome.

'Everything OK?' Steven asked with concern. His deep blue eyes perused her figure, taking in her change of clothes. Slowly, they roved over her legs, paused briefly in the middle, before rising to her breasts, and then once again met her gaze.

'Sure,' she replied, her voice husky and intimate from his blatant visual caress.

Their eyes held for another second before Steven closed the gap between them, gathering Vicky into his arms. His lips met hers in a searing kiss that rocked the firm foundations she'd so carefully built up. His tongue plunged into her mouth as his hands travelled down her back to cup her denim-clad *derrière*.

The heat of his body scorched through her and Vicky wound her arms about his neck, urging his mouth to continue its onslaught. Matching his hunger, that only seemed to increase the magnetism surrounding them.

Steven pushed her gently backwards and soon she felt the bed pressing into the back of her knees. She eased herself down, never once letting his mouth break contact with hers, and soon his body was covering hers completely, his desire for her all too evident.

Reaching one hand between them, Steven tugged her T-shirt from her waistband. When his warm hand met her flesh she gasped, arching her back to meet him. With agonising slowness, his fingers travelled up her body, finally finding their goal.

Vicky tore her mouth from his and groaned out loud as his hand cupped her breast. She felt as if she were on fire—all over. Every part of her being—soul, mind and body—wanted this man. She wanted him—now and for ever.

Steven trailed hot kisses down her neck and around her collar-bone. He raised his head to look down into her face.

The desire in their eyes was mutual. Breathing in deeply, he whispered, 'Vicky…'

She closed her eyes, waiting for his lips to meet hers, but instead she shivered at the sudden withdrawal of his body as he leapt from the bed and disappeared into the hallway.

Vicky lay still for a moment, wondering again at his abrupt departure from their love-making. Then, she also smelt it.

Clambering off the bed, Vicky quickly tucked her T-shirt back into her jeans and followed Steven into the kitchen.

'Damage report?' she asked as she came to stand beside him.

'Salvageable but only just.' He turned and smiled down into her face. 'Dinner is ready.'

Vicky looked at the burnt offering and burst out laughing, her previous apprehension disappearing into thin air. 'Let's eat!'

She quickly made the salad while Steven took care of the other preparations, and soon they were halfway through the meal.

'So how's Fred? I presume you saw him again, before coming home?' Vicky asked.

'Yes, I did. He's nicely stabilised. I'm very happy with his progress. Nicole has set up a bed for Dorothy in the ward, which made Fred happy. Ninety-seven years old and his heart's still as strong as that of an ox. I have a feeling he'll make a complete recovery and my reservations at performing the total hip replacement have eased somewhat.'

'Good. Hey,' she said, gesturing to the steaks, 'this is quite good. Even if it *is* a little overdone.'

'I'm a bachelor.' He shrugged as though that explained it all.

'Meaning…what? That you always burn your food?' Vicky teased.

Steven smiled. 'Only when I'm…distracted.' He gave her a wolfish grin and Vicky almost choked on her food.

'That's not…exactly what I meant.'

'No? Are you surprised I can cook?'

'Yes,' she answered frankly as she took a sip of her wine. 'Most of the men I've…er…' She stopped as she realised he could easily have misinterpreted what she'd been about to say.

'Most of the men you've dated,' he supplied, encouraging her to continue.

'Uh, yes. Well, most of them couldn't cook at all. They expected it to be the woman's job.'

'Even when you work such long hours? Tut-tut. How insensitive of them.'

'Exactly.'

'I'm different,' he announced.

'So I've noticed.'

'I can cook. I can clean and I can even sew.'

'You forget, Mr Pearce, that I've already witnessed your sewing ability. I'm sure Fred will also be pleased with your…home-making skills.'

'I've never had any complaints from previous patients,' he stated matter-of-factly, reaching over and pinching a baby tomato off her plate.

'Hey,' she objected, but was too late to slap his hand. Steven gave her a schoolboy grin and she laughed. As she finished her meal she tried to remember when she'd last felt this happy.

Over coffee, they sat back in the comfortable lounge chair and watched Cary Grant in *She Done Him Wrong*.

'My whole family loves the old black and whites,' Steven whispered in her ear as he placed an arm around her shoulders. His breath on her neck and the touch of his body against hers were almost her undoing. However, she forced herself to relax and enjoy being close to a man she was coming to care for very deeply.

She cleared her throat and whispered, 'So do I. Especially this one. Mae West is a riot!'

When the movie was finished, Vicky was content to stay exactly where she was. Steven's arm was still around her, drawing her close to him.

'Comfortable?' he asked, and she nodded. 'I'm sorry, Vicky, but I need to move. Nature calls.'

Vicky allowed herself to be untangled and watched as he left the room. Stretching her body, she yawned and closed her eyes for a moment. She heard Steven come back into the room but didn't open her eyes.

She felt him draw near and her anticipation grew so that when his lips finally pressed themselves gently against hers she simply melted. When Steven had finished the kiss she opened her eyes and looked up at him.

'Thanks,' he said. 'I've had a great evening. Being in the city, someone always calls around or invariably the phone—'

He didn't even get to finish his sentence before the telephone beside them shrilled to life. They both groaned. Steven picked it up and Vicky tried to ignore the stab of annoyance at him for answering it the second time that day. She was having a good time with him and shouldn't let her annoyance at his high-handedness ruin a perfect evening.

When he didn't hand the receiver over, she realised the call was for him. Listening unashamedly, Vicky frowned at his words.

'Is there a note in his file anywhere about this?' he asked the caller.

'Fred?' she asked softly, and he nodded.

'Then change the antibiotic to erythromycin,' he ordered. 'Hopefully, that will help stop his nausea and vomiting. Does he have a skin rash?' Steven waited for the answer.

'Then monitor him closely and let me know if one appears. If you hand me over to another registered nurse, the telephone order can be confirmed.'

Steven waited for a moment, before repeating the change of drug instructions. It was standard procedure for two RNs to receive a telephone drug order, thereby ensuring a safeguard. 'I'll authorise the drugs on his chart when I do a round tomorrow morning.' He paused. 'No. I'll be in before seven a.m., Sister. See you then.' He rang off.

'I take it Fred had a problem with the antibiotics?'

'Yes.' Steven ran a hand along his jaw. 'Apparently amoxicillin doesn't agree with him. He's vomited and had a bit of diarrhoea but hopefully changing him to erythromycin will clear that up and continue to stave off any infection.' He paused for a moment, before saying, 'The night sister sounds very competent.'

'All of our staff are, Mr Pearce.' Vicky couldn't resist teasing him. 'Judith Tedesco. She and her husband both work nights at the hospital—have done since their last child left the nest. Both are excellent registered nurses.' Vicky cleared her throat and asked, 'Do you need to go in so early?'

'Yes. I'm needed back in Adelaide tomorrow. I only came today to check out the status of the cottage.'

'I'm glad you did...uh...for Fred's sake,' she added, when he gave her an enquiring look.

'Of course,' he replied, as though he didn't believe her. Steven studied her for a moment, before saying, 'What if that call had been for you? An emergency.'

'You would have handed the receiver over and I would have dealt with it,' she answered, starting to feel a little on edge at the tone in his voice.

'You know what I mean. I still don't think you've given enough consideration to travelling time and patient outcome. It would have taken you a good five minutes to put your shoes on, collect your bag and keys and get into the car, not to mention the fifteen-minute drive to the hospital.'

'Haven't we discussed this before?' Vicky asked, trying to keep her tone light. If what Mary had said was true, if Steven was fishing to see if she'd move closer to town, then perhaps this was her chance to find out. You'd better not blow your top, Hansen, or you may never know.

Steven ploughed on as if she hadn't spoken. His tone was earnest as though he were trying to make a child see reason. 'You've been trained in primary trauma care and stabilisation. You know the first few minutes are *vital* to the patient's well-being. Whether they live or die.'

'And most of those first few minutes are given at the crash site.' She placed a hand on his arm. 'I understand what you're saying, Steven, but I can't be *everywhere*—*all* the time.'

'But if you lived closer to the hospital, you'd be ready and waiting when the patient arrived. Not still driving to reach them.'

Vicky removed her hand, held her breath and counted to five, before saying, 'Why are you so determined on this point?'

'I'm simply pointing out the fact that as the only general practitioner for miles it would be better if you lived closer to the facilities that provided the care.'

'We have very well-trained staff. All our nurses, as well as Mac, of course, are kept up to date on any new techniques in primary trauma care.'

'That's all well and good but *you* are the doctor. *You* are the one who can prescribe the medicines and perform the techniques.'

Vicky counted to ten this time and smiled. 'What about you?'

'What about me?' He frowned.

'You are the district's new orthopaedic surgeon. You will

be required more than I will to attend crash victims and other primary trauma cases. You have not only the skills but the qualifications to perform such life-saving miracles. How come you've chosen to stay at the cottage? The distance is just as far as this place.'

'The cottage isn't a permanent arrangement,' he said and Vicky's heart grew wings at his words. 'It's only a stopgap until I see how things work out down here.' The wings disappeared.

'But still,' she persisted, 'even with that being the case, shouldn't you live closer to the hospital? Stopgap or not, accidents still happen. Shouldn't you practise what you preach?'

'I was planning on moving closer, yes, but that's not the point.'

'What is your point?' she asked, feeling the wings begin to grow again. At least he was going to stay—that was a start. Could she dare hope that perhaps one day…one day they might have more permanence in each other's lives?

'This house.' He spread his arms wide.

'What's wrong with my house?' she asked, starting to get edgy.

'There's nothing *wrong* with it except that it's far too big for you.'

Vicky stared at him in disbelief. She counted to twenty, before replying. 'This is my home. Where I grew up. I don't see it as being too big or too small. The familiarity, the memories—they're all here. Like these bookshelves.' She indicated the floor-to-ceiling shelves which were overflowing with books. 'My grandfather built those shelves before my father was born. That chair was my mother's favourite. The crockery in the display cabinet over there was my parents' wedding gift from Fred and Dorothy. This may be just a big old house to you, but to me it's full of irreplaceable memories. I love it and I need it in my life. It's who I am, Steven. Can you understand that?'

'Yes, but when are you going to create some memories of your own?'

'I don't need to move house to do that. I can add to the memories that are already here. This house was built to be a home and that's what it is. I hope that one day my children will fill these rooms with laughter and happiness. The way it used to be.'

'But what about now? You don't have children but you do have patients who need their doctor. You told me yourself the main reason you returned to practise medicine here was to serve the people you grew up with. There are people waiting to pay generously for your land. Aren't you being a little bit selfish by refusing point-blank to move closer to the hospital?'

Vicky was past the point of counting. '*Selfish?* Just who do you think you are, Steven Pearce?' She rose to her feet and planted her hands firmly on her hips. If Steven didn't realise she was angry, he was about to find out.

'If…*if* I ever moved from this house, closer to the hospital, as you suggest, there is no way I would ever sell it. I'd rent it out because one day my children *will* be in these rooms, learning and appreciating the history that is evident in every single nook and cranny of these walls.

'How can you even suggest that I move when one third of the land has already been sold by my sister and soon my brother will sell also. This is the only plot left of our heritage and, with Nigel Fairweather and the Sharlock Wine Company circling around like vultures, there is no way I *could* leave and there is absolutely nothing that could induce me to sell.'

She took a deep breath and lowered her voice. 'You really have some nerve to waltz into my home as a guest and make such an issue out of something that is none of your business.

I don't care how much money Fairweather or that wine company offer me, it would never be able to replace my history, my heritage and my home.

'Right now, I'm going to bed. As you have an early trip to Adelaide tomorrow, I'll no doubt see you on your return.'

With that Vicky spun on her heel and marched out of the room, resisting the urge to slam her bedroom door. The man made her furious. She paced around her room, trying to concentrate on breathing exercises which she hoped would calm her down.

So much for Mary's theory. Steven Pearce wasn't interested in her as a prospective wife. What on earth had she been thinking?

It was another half-hour before Vicky was able to pick up the ever-present medical journal from her bedside table and concentrate on the words, then another half-hour before she was completely absorbed in the article and yet another before she was sound asleep.

Steven put his hands into his pockets and shrugged as Vicky stormed out of the room. That hadn't gone quite as he'd planned. Instead of gently persuading her to think about alternative accommodation, he'd only succeeding in making her angry and upset—again!

He walked over to the window and looked out into the darkness of night. Did he really believe his own arguments? That she wasn't providing adequate care for her patients by living so far away from the hospital?

He'd witnessed for himself that day Vicky's competence, not only in the operating theatre but in dealing with her patients and colleagues. She was extremely good.

Steven closed the curtains and walked out of the room, switching off the light as he went. The hall light was on as well so he also switched that off, after checking that the back and front doors were both locked.

He stopped outside Vicky's bedroom door, his hand raised to knock, an apology on his lips. He listened for a moment and could hear her pacing around the room, muttering to herself. Perhaps now was not the best time to make an appearance.

He made his way through the darkened house, marvelling at how much darker it was in the country than the city, to his allocated room. A smile touched his lips as he recalled the look on her face when she'd entered with the sheets and towels and had seen him stripped to the waist.

But having moved into her house so he could be closer to her and therefore have more opportunity to induce her to sell, Steven felt he was definitely complicating matters with his own conduct.

He decided then and there to forget about inducing her to sell. After all, money wasn't everything—but Victoria Hansen might be…

She was becoming an enigma to him, and one which he felt deserved further exploration. At this precise moment in time he couldn't care less if she sold this house or not. The Sharlock Wine Company stood to make a hefty sum of money just by owning the other two parcels of land. They didn't really *need* Vicky's share.

What he *did* care about, however, were her uninhibited reactions to himself. No other woman had ever offered him such abandonment in her kisses and it was affecting him far too deeply for his liking.

CHAPTER EIGHT

'GOOD girl, Megan,' Vicky praised the four-and-a-half-year-old girl who was bravely trying not to cry. 'One more on the other side,' she said, quickly swabbing and carefully inserting the needle into Megan's arm. 'All done. You're so brave. I think that deserves a lollipop, don't you?'

Megan nodded her head, her eyes filling with tears, but she was determined not to cry. Her mother carefully picked her up off the examination couch where she'd been sitting very still, and gave her a big hug and kiss.

Vicky reached for her lolly jar, thankful the day was almost over. Monday clinics were always so busy. Thank goodness she only had one more patient to go.

'What colour would you like?' Vicky asked as she held the jar out to Megan.

'Red, please.' Megan held out her hand to receive the treat.

'Do I just watch for the usual side effects or have there been some developments in the past few years since she had her last lot of immunisations?' Sonya McMahon asked.

'She may get a temperature and slight swelling at the needle site but, apart from that, just give her lots of cuddles and kisses for the next twenty-four hours. The immunisation drugs have radically improved since Megan was eighteen months old, which was when she had her last set, so I'd be very surprised if she did get a temperature. If you're worried at any time, give me a call and I'll come right out.'

'Thanks, Vicky.' Sonya turned her attention to Megan. 'That's all, darling,' she said soothingly. 'Let's go tell Daddy what a brave girl you've been.'

When they'd left her consulting room, Vicky quickly wrote up the notes, thankful that most of the mothers in the district believed in immunising their children.

When she was ready, Vicky buzzed Trudy to signal she was ready for Susie Hartford. A few seconds later the door opened and fifteen-year-old Susie and her mother walked in.

After they'd sat down on the other side of her desk, Vicky enquired, 'What can I do for you today?'

'We need a repeat prescription for her inhalers,' Mrs Hartford said. 'Also, with this being spring—the silly season, as most asthmatic suffers call it—she's been a little bit worse than usual.'

After listening to the girl's chest, Vicky reached into the cupboard for her peak flow meter. She held the device out to Susie, who had used it so often there was no need for instructions. Placing the mouthpiece between her lips, she breathed in deeply and then pushed the air out of her lungs as hard as she could. The device had three compartments, with a plastic ball in each. The idea was to raise all three balls to the top of their compartments with one breath— Susie raised only the first one, the other two didn't move.

'When did you take your last puff of Ventolin?'

'About an hour ago,' Susie replied, a slight wheeze in her voice. She coughed a little, then took three deep breaths, concentrating on relaxing.

'Take another puff now and try to raise the second ball,' Vicky urged.

Susie did as she was asked and was successful in raising the second ball.

'Excellent,' Vicky replied. 'Nebuliser?'

'Every night,' Mrs Hartford assured her.

'Right.' Vicky nodded and reached for her prescription pad. 'I'd like Susie to increase her dosage on the nebuliser as that's the preventative medication, which should help ease the need to use the Ventolin more during the day. I presume you're cleaning and keeping her room as free from dust mites as possible?'

'As always,' Mrs Hartford replied. 'A real pain in the neck but it really helps.'

'Good.' Vicky handed the prescriptions over. 'I'd like to see you again at the end of next week and we'll see how the increased dose of the nebuliser is working,' she said to Susie.

'Thanks, Dr Hansen,' Susie said with a smile before she and her mother left the room.

Vicky sagged into her chair and let her arms go limp the instant the door was closed. Monday clinic—over and done with. Now she could concentrate on the evening ahead.

Being alone with Steven.

Not that she'd seen him all that much over the weekend, but he'd been constantly in her thoughts.

On Saturday morning, Vicky had stumbled sleepily into the kitchen to find him eating a bowl of cereal. Because she'd thought he'd already gone, she hadn't bothered to put her robe over her thigh-length T-shirt.

'Good morning.' His tone had been seductive, as his eyes had roved over her long legs. Vicky's body tingled at the memory of how his eyes could melt her to the ground, even when she was still mad at him.

'You look gorgeous when you're half-awake.'

Feeling embarrassed yet flattered by his compliments, Vicky had managed to pull herself together and brush them away as she would have an annoying fly.

'I thought you'd left.'

'Apparently not.'

'Then shouldn't you be on your way? Fred will be waiting.'

'Still mad at me, I see.' He'd smiled a slow and aggravating smile as he'd advanced towards her. 'You leave me no option.'

'What do you mean?'

'If you're still cross about our little discussion last night, then I'll have to fix things before I go.'

'Fix what?'

'Your attitude towards me. I can't very well leave you for a few days, knowing you'll stew and dissect every word I've said against your home.'

'Why not?'

'Because I'm a compassionate man. Those kinds of thoughts aren't worth wasting brain power over.' He'd walked over to stand in front of her, forcing her to lean back against the bench, effectively trapping her.

His hands had slowly run up her arms, coming to rest on her shoulders. Vicky closed her eyes, remembering the sensations he'd evoked. Forcing her to meet his gaze, he'd said, 'Don't be mad at me, Vic.' Then he'd lowered his head and kissed her.

Feeling her heartbeat accelerate, she relived every touch, every tantalising kiss, the way his hands felt as they'd gathered her closer, the scent of his aftershave and the power he still possessed over her.

Oh, she had stewed and dissected after he'd finished the earth-shattering kiss and said goodbye, but not about their argument. When she'd gone to bed on Saturday, after completing the hospital work, the weekly home visits and catching up on paperwork, Vicky had lain awake, remembering everything about him and how he made her feel.

Throughout Sunday he'd been her constant companion as she'd pottered around her house and garden, able for the first time in weeks to get some odd jobs done as there had been no emergencies.

She'd actually found herself *thinking* about his comments—insinuating she could give better care if she lived closer to the hospital—without getting all steamed up and angry. As a doctor, she'd been trained to assess all the options before making a final decision. Perhaps Steven had had a valid point?

She'd looked around at the garden she was weeding, then out to the rolling pastures of her land and beyond, and had known he was wrong. *This* was where she belonged.

If her surprise on finding him still home on Saturday morning had been great, it had been multiplied when she'd found breakfast prepared and waiting for her on the kitchen table this morning. Coffee, orange juice and a bowl of cereal awaited her. An identical place had been set opposite and a handsome doctor dressed in a navy suit had greeted her.

'I trust you slept well?'

'You're here!' she blurted out.

'No, it's just a figment of your imagination.' He gave her a sardonic grin.

'I… It's just…that I didn't hear you come home last night.'

'Waiting up for me?'

'Well, I wasn't sure when to expect you,' she said huffily, and sat down.

'So you *were* waiting up for me.'

When she didn't answer, he volunteered, 'I didn't get in until after two a.m. You were sound asleep so I decided to surprise you.'

'Out partying, were you?' The thought of him having fun with someone else sent a sharp spiral of pain through her.

'Careful. Your claws are showing,' he teased. 'I was all ready to leave when I received a call from my brother-in-law.'

Vicky's concern was instant. 'Is everything all right?'

'Yes. Kathryn had a bit of cramping, but after an ultrasound and a blood test, which showed that everything was fine, they sent her home.'

'How far is she?'

'Just over twenty-eight weeks.'

'If she's having cramps now, she'd better take it easy.'

'That's what Jack keeps telling her. He's so possessive of Kath and this baby…but after everything he's been through, that awful time in Africa, I believe he has the right.'

'I'm glad she's OK.'

'You and me both. Now, we'd better eat breakfast or risk running overtime on our clinics.'

'Your first clinic. Nervous?'

'Me? Never!'

'I'd believe that.'

'Good. Now eat.'

The conversation was kept light and impersonal throughout the meal but as they left the house together and Steven walked Vicky to her car, he pulled her into his arms.

'Did you miss me?' He lowered his head and kissed her softly.

Vicky closed her eyes, her body singing at his light and gentle touch as she responded.

'I'll take that as a yes,' he said huskily when they finally drew apart. 'Off to work.'

Vicky opened her eyes, her heart pounding at the remembrance and anticipation of his touch. Placing her head in her hands, she mumbled, 'You're a mess, Hansen. The guy has you tied up in so many knots, you're all ajumble.'

She was happy with him one minute, mad at him the next. Never having experienced this before, Vicky was having trouble controlling the see-saw of her emotions, but of one thing she was certain. She couldn't wait to get home and see him again.

Quickly writing up Susie Hartford's notes, Vicky tidied her desk and made plans to make Steven dinner. After all, it was her turn. As her cooking skills weren't all that great, she decided to go for a trusty, no-fail meal of spaghetti Bolognese.

Dumping the day's files on Trudy's desk, Vicky said goodbye, leaving the receptionist to lock up, then hurried to the shops.

When Steven arrived home, she had everything under control—except her racing heartbeat.

'Thank you for dinner,' he said as they sat down in the lounge room.

'You're welcome.' Vicky sat with her back straight and rigid, unsure what to do next. A movie, like the other night? Discuss an article she'd read yesterday in one of her journals? Talk? It was only eight-thirty—too early to go to bed.

Their conversation during dinner had been kept to common topics such as how their clinics had been, how Fred was progressing—generic things. Vicky felt unsure but it was an excited something's-going-to-happen-soon type of unsureness. It was as though she were in a holding pattern high in the sky, waiting to have word that soon terra firma would be beneath her once more.

She realised Steven was looking at her, concern on his face. Reaching out a hand, he felt the muscle between her shoulder and neck.

'What have you been doing, Dr Hansen? Your trapezius is as tight as a drum. Turn around,' he ordered, and she swivelled so her back was to him.

The feel of his warm hands through her cotton shirt caused even more tension knots.

'Relax,' he whispered, and Vicky closed her eyes, finally submitting to his request. Concentrating on her breathing rather than on Steven's touch, she soon began to feel the tension slip from her.

His technique had her turning to jelly after five minutes. Vicky was definitely relaxing but it was when she heard him exhale slowly, almost painfully, that her senses began to return.

He'd shifted his weight more evenly so one leg was along the couch and the other on the floor. Vicky was sitting between them. If she leaned back slightly, she'd be resting against his firm, muscled chest, feeling the heat of his body, knowing that he would lower his head and nibble her neck. His hands would stop their massaging and instead they'd explore her body with the same sweeping strokes.

She shivered involuntarily at the mental scenario and began wondering whether things would really be so bad if she allowed herself to conduct an affair with Steven.

Could she play with fire and not get burned? Would he rip her heart out and keep it for ever? Was it time to take some chances?

Steven might not be the marrying kind but did that really matter? Yes. To her, it mattered a great deal, she realised. Although Steven sent her into an emotional frenzy whenever he was near, in the long run it wouldn't be enough.

She wanted it all. The romance, the love, the passion, the dependability, the friendship, the soul-mate. Steven really only offered the passion, fiery though it was. Could Vicky risk her future happiness just for that? How long would it be before the attraction they felt towards each other petered out, leaving them hollow, with nothing in common?

No. An affair was out of the question and, to be fair, she must tell him how she felt.

'What are you thinking about?' His voice was so sensuous that Vicky almost capitulated.

'You're not going to like it,' she whispered.

'I don't think I am either.' He stopped massaging and turned her to face him. 'You've started to tense up again.'

'It's this.' She looked into his eyes, hoping to find the right words. 'You and me.'

'Go on,' he prompted.

Vicky took a deep breath and plunged right in. 'I can't have an affair with you, Steven.' She noticed his lips twitching at the corners. 'And if you make a crack, saying you weren't offering one, I'll get really mad.' She sighed. 'This is hard enough for me to say without your teasing.'

'Very well.' He nodded, his face sombre.

'I…like you but it's not enough. I need someone who will be here for me—for ever. I want to get married and have children. I—'

'Think too much,' he interrupted. 'Vicky, let's just take things one step at a time.' He leaned forward and placed a brief kiss on her lips. 'And it's my professional opinion that you need some R and R. Why don't you make some fresh coffee and I'll choose a video?'

'OK.' Vicky sighed and went into the kitchen. Performing the familiar task, it allowed her to think about what she'd said. Had she made an even bigger mess of things? No, she didn't think so. The atmosphere prior to her speech had been charged with sexual electricity and Vicky knew, all too well, where they would have ended up.

If they'd made love, she knew he'd have complete control over her heart—and that privilege she was only willing to hand to her future husband.

Determined not to feel awkward, Vicky decided to take Steven's advice. One step at a time was enough for now, and at least he knew where she stood on the issue. There was no doubt in her mind that he was attracted to her. She'd seen his desire often enough in the smouldering depths of his blue eyes.

Time. They both needed time.

When the coffee was ready, she returned to the lounge room to find him relaxing on the couch, television on and remote control in his hand.

'Isn't this what every guy dreams of?' she quipped as she handed Steven a cup. 'Someone bringing him coffee and possession of the remote control.'

He smiled and pressed the play button. He'd chosen *The*

Fugitive and Vicky knew why. There was no romance and not even a hint of sexual tension throughout the film.

'I didn't realise you had such a vast collection of videos,' he remarked as they watched the beginning.

'It's how I relax,' she replied, starting to become absorbed in Harrison Ford's brilliant acting.

When the movie was finished, Steven pulled Vicky to her feet. 'Time for bed.'

At her sudden intake of breath, he clarified, 'I did understand what you said earlier so you have no need to worry. We both need a good night's sleep.'

'Aren't you going to Victor Harbour tomorrow?' she asked, wondering whether he was going to kiss her goodnight or simply turn away and go into his room. Although she'd said she didn't want an affair, that didn't necessarily mean she wouldn't welcome his kisses.

'Yes. I'll stay overnight as I have my first operating session down there on Wednesday as well. I spoke with the nursing administrator today and she said both the clinic and list are fully booked.'

'That's good news for you. See how much your services are needed?'

The unintentional *double entendre* of her words made them both stare into each other's eyes before Steven gave in to a slow and seductive smile. His arms came around her and she rested her head on his chest.

'Victoria Hansen,' he said with a rich laugh, 'I don't think you know *what* you want at this point in time.' Steven looked down at her and bent his head to kiss her waiting lips.

The kiss was…lovely. Neither passionate nor platonic. It was the type of kiss designed to allow one to dream wonderful dreams and sleep soundly all night. How had he known that was exactly what she needed?

'I'll see you on Wednesday some time,' he said softly

when they finally broke apart. 'Goodnight and sweet dreams.'

On Wednesday morning Vicky was woken by the telephone. Her first thought was that something terrible had happened to Steven. Quickly she reached out for the receiver.

'Vicky Hansen.' Glancing at the clock, she saw it was five-thirty. It had to be bad news.

'Vicky…' It was Daniel. A prickle of apprehension worked its way over her body at his tone. 'I need you at Molly's house immediately.'

'What's wrong?' she asked as she clambered out of bed and started changing her clothes.

'Our not-so-friendly neighbourhood junkie decided to pay another visit to Molly's home. Unfortunately, this time she disturbed him while he was rifling her drug cupboard.'

'Is she all right?'

'He came at her with a knife, cutting her arm before he managed to escape in her car. I've notified the other police stations but it's doubtful we'll catch up with him.'

'When did all this happen?'

'About twenty minutes ago. Molly refuses to leave the house and has managed to put a temporary bandage on her arm, but I'm positive it needs stitching. Should I send for Mac?'

'Not yet. I'd like to see Molly first and, besides, I live closer than Mac. I'm leaving right now.' Vicky hung up and gathered her medical bag and keys, before rushing out to her car.

When she reached Molly's farm it was lit up like a Christmas tree. Every light was on and there were a few vehicles parked out front. Pulling up beside Frank Mitchell's truck, Vicky realised the locals were once again rallying around their own in time of need.

Daniel was organising people to look for clues as, again,

there was no sign of forced entry. Frank's wife Mavis was in the kitchen, making preparations for breakfast. She gave Vicky a smile.

'Good morning to you, dear. Molly's in her bedroom and quite shaken up, poor girl. Go and fix her up and put her to rights. I'll bring you both in a warm drink soon enough.'

Vicky did as she was told and found Molly sitting on top of the bedcover, leaning back against the wall, her eyes closed as she cradled her injured arm. Vicky knocked softly on the open door, trying not to startle the vet who had tears flowing down her cheeks. Vicky quickly entered the room and reached for a tissue.

'Hey, Molly.' Vicky wiped the tears away. 'Everything's going to be fine.'

Molly slowly opened her eyes and looked sadly at her friend. 'It was so scary. He was so aggressive that I'm lucky to only have a cut arm.' She lowered her eyes. 'I've never seen anyone so obsessed before. Then again, I've never met a drug-user before.'

'All they think about is their next fix,' Vicky agreed quietly. 'When they're high they're usually mellow, but when they start to come out of it, with no other means of getting back into their euphoric state, they can be violent and dangerous people. I wish there was something I could do to help you through this, other than offering to be here when you need someone to lean on…' Vicky sighed. 'But for now, let me see to your arm.'

The wound was quite deep and, as Daniel had surmised, it needed quite a few stitches. Vicky gave Molly a local anaesthetic before she began to suture the wound but Molly refused any other type of analgesics to help her through the pain.

'Come on,' Vicky urged after she'd bandaged the arm. 'If a similar wound had been on one of your animals, you'd have prescribed painkillers for when the anaesthetic wore off. The owners of the animal would administer them as per your instructions and the animal would make a better recovery. I know you're up to date with your injections but I'd still like you to take a course of antibiotics to stave off any infection.' After all, Vicky added silently, they had no idea where that knife had been.

Mavis gave a knock on the door and came in, carrying a tray of food and drink.

'Have some tea and toast,' she urged Molly. 'I've brought coffee for you, Vicky, but Molly gets a cup of sickly sweet tea. My mother swore by it,' she added for emphasis.

'Thanks, but I'm not hungry,' Molly replied.

'I'm not giving you a choice,' Mavis retorted in her best schoolmarm voice. 'You'll eat at least one piece of toast and drink all that tea even if I have to force every last drop down your throat. Tell her, Vicky.'

Vicky smiled at Molly, hoping to lift the other woman's spirits. 'I doubt she'd do it,' she said, giving Mavis a wink, 'but, then again, I wouldn't want to test her. It will do you good because once you've eaten I'd like you to sleep. You're exhausted, Molly, and that will only add to your shock and stress if you don't relax now. Come on,' Vicky said, reaching for a piece of toast. 'I'll join you.' She took a bite and reached for the coffee. 'Just what the doctor ordered,' she remarked, and finally received a small smile from Molly in return. It wasn't a huge one, just a slight upward turn at the corners of her mouth.

'I guess you're both going to bother me until I do as I'm told,' she said resignedly, and both Mavis and Vicky nodded.

Vicky stayed for the next hour or so, keeping a close eye on Molly as she eventually fell into a restless sleep. Daniel was still conducting his investigation, leaving no stone unturned, and Mavis was supplying food for the hungry helpers.

By around eight-thirty Vicky was satisfied with Molly's condition and, leaving her in Mavis's capable hands, headed for home. As she drove past Jerome's property she noticed a small group of men doing a survey on the land. Her spirits slumped as she realised it wouldn't be too long before another part of her family history would slip away into an outsider's hands.

'If only I had the money,' she said out loud. But her world wasn't founded on if onlys.

Dragging her weary body inside, she reached for the phone and tried to call her brother but instead she had to leave a message on his answering machine. No doubt he wouldn't return her calls as this was one topic they would never agree on.

It all suddenly became too much for her. She was worried about Molly, concerned that a junkie was still loose in their district and now there were strangers ready to do as they wished with her family's land.

She wished Steven were back so she could lean on him, feel his arms around her, holding her securely in their embrace. Even with their differing opinions about her land, it didn't matter.

Vicky realised she was coming to depend on Steven Pearce far more than she ought.

'Any coffee left?' Steven asked from behind her.

Vicky pivoted in her chair, a smile on her face. 'Hi. Yes, there is. Come and have a cup.' She was so glad to see him. The past few days had been long and lonely and she'd been surprised at just how much she'd missed him.

He'd returned from Victor Harbour late on Wednesday evening and had left early on Thursday morning for his private clinic and operating list in the city. Then she'd received a call from him between operating cases, telling her he wouldn't be back until this morning.

To say she'd been disappointed was an understatement. Although she'd panicked about having him in the house overnight, due to her uncontrollable libido, it was nothing compared to the desolation she felt when he wasn't there at all.

Vicky had never minded the solitude of living alone before, but now that Steven had been in her house, watching television, sharing meals, kissing her goodnight, the solitude wasn't the same.

Her eyes devoured him as he walked over to the coffee-pot. He was dressed casually in those snug-fitting denim jeans and a white polo shirt. Vicky's heart zoomed into overdrive and she closed her eyes in an attempt to shut out the sight of him and control her breathing.

'Are you OK?' he asked, sitting down opposite her.

Her eyes snapped open. 'I'm fine,' she answered, a little too quickly, chiding herself for behaving like a schoolgirl.

'How are you enjoying your morning off?'

Vicky cleared her throat and was happy her voice sounded normal. 'Like I always do. I sleep in a little, take longer in the shower and have a leisurely breakfast. When that's all done, it's usually time to go to work.'

'The story of our lives,' he joked. 'Why don't you tell me what's been happening over the past few days? You mentioned briefly on Wednesday night about the vet—Molly isn't it? How's she doing?'

'She's coping. The fact that Daniel has no leads on this junkie still has her rattled but, then, the whole town's rattled by the incident. Frank and Mavis are staying with her. Mavis is Molly's aunt.'

'How long will they be staying?'

'Probably for a few weeks. They're using it as an excuse to have their own house painted. I think that's so Molly will accept having them around.'

'If they need somewhere to stay, she's happy to oblige.'

'Precisely.'

Steven gave her a smile. 'You country folk are just such hospitable people.'

'You should know,' Vicky replied, her voice thick with meaning. Her words caused the atmosphere around them to change and she once again became all too aware of him. Her tongue darted between her lips, moistening them against their sudden dryness.

'H-how's Fred? I suppose you've been to see him this morning?' Vicky asked, unable to shift her gaze from his mouth. She saw his lips move when he spoke but didn't hear a word.

The butterflies that seemed to be living permanently in her stomach took flight once more as her mind recalled the last time his lips had been pressed against hers. How she wished he would repeat the action—immediately.

'Vicky?' His voice was as smooth as silk and her eyes managed to dart up to meet his. 'You haven't heard a word I've—' He broke off as he read the burning need in her expression.

Reaching out for her hand, Steven held it tenderly as he pulled her gently towards him. Vicky slowly stood and came around the table. When she was in front of him he tugged her down onto his lap, wrapping his arms around her securely.

'How remiss of me,' he murmured. 'Not saying hello to you properly.'

'Stop talking and ki—'

Steven did as she asked and kissed her, effectively eliminating the request.

It was all Vicky had remembered and more. Their craving for each other was definitely becoming more pronounced each time they were together like this. Steven held her tightly as his first subtle kisses became more ardent and probing.

From the depths of her soul Vicky felt a rush of love rise up and envelop her, allowing her to give herself completely to Steven. The fire burning within her showed itself through the pressure of her lips, the pleasure she derived from him and the pulsations of her heart.

Love? Steven Pearce?

Vicky broke away from him, slipping out of his grasp. She stood before him, her breathing rapid and uneven. It was true! Her feelings were completely true! She was in love with Steven Pearce.

A look of shock must have been on her face because instantly Steven got up.

'Vicky? What's wrong?'

It took her a moment to answer and when she did her voice was a whisper. 'N-nothing. I…just…' she stammered, then stopped, not knowing what to say. The grandfather clock in the hall chimed eleven-thirty and Vicky reached for an excuse.

'Is that the time? I'd better get ready for my clinic. You've got Fred's operation this afternoon and Nicole would shoot me if I allowed you to be late. We'd better hustle.'

Vicky knew she was babbling but her sole thought was to escape from Steven's overwhelming presence to the sanctuary of her room where she could slowly begin to analyse her feelings.

Pivoting on her heel, she all but ran from the room, shutting her door firmly behind her. She rested against the door for an instant, before crossing to the mirror. Taking a good look at her face, she realised the truth.

Vicky shook her head in denial but her heart refused to let her do such a cowardly thing. She loved him. She loved Steven Pearce with every fibre of her being and there was absolutely nothing she could do about it.

CHAPTER NINE

FRED'S total hip replacement operation was accomplished without complication. Or so Steven told Vicky when he called the news through to her clinic late that afternoon. Up until that time, she'd had every patient asking for news.

'Fred was stable throughout,' he reported, his deep voice making her heart rate accelerate. 'He's in Recovery at the moment and Emma appears happy with his progress as well.'

'Great news. I'll make sure I pass it on.' Vicky was amazed at how controlled she sounded.

'Good. How's the clinic?'

'Full. I'm running an hour late as it is and I've still got five or six patients to go.'

'I know exactly how you feel.' His rich laugh echoed down the phone, causing a shiver of excitement to course through her body.

'Looks as though I'll be finished before you so I guess it's my turn to cook dinner,' he continued.

Vicky thought about another meal and evening together— especially since the recent discovery of her true feelings— and wondered how she'd cope. If she'd had trouble saying no to Steven before, it would be impossible now.

'Sure,' she agreed. 'See you then— Oh, and thanks for letting me know about Fred.'

Vicky rang off and buried her face in her hands. Steven even had the ability to affect her over the phone. There was no hope for her, literally none. This love-sickness was here to stay and there was no cure.

Vicky managed to finish just before seven o'clock and,

after rushing through her dictation, said goodnight to Trudy and hurried home. She was anxious to see Steven again but dreading it at the same time.

When Vicky walked in the back door, the wonderful aroma of roast chicken assailed her. She walked into the kitchen to find Steven sharpening the knife, ready to carve the chicken.

'Perfect timing.' He smiled and Vicky's insides turned to mush. She leaned against the bench, thankful for its support. Steven took the opportunity to plant a brief kiss on her lips, before continuing his task.

Vicky's heart contracted at his thoughtful gesture and her love intensified.

'I don't require your assistance tonight so why don't you pour the wine and sit down?' He gestured to the table which was set for two, with a bottle of local white wine chilling in an ice bucket.

Vicky did as Steven suggested and waited for him to serve the meal. Feeling the tension begin to drain out of her, she listened as he told her anecdotes from his past.

'Kathryn was asking about you yesterday. I caught up with her and Jack for lunch before my operating list,' he explained.

'How does your sister know about me?'

'I'd already told her where I was staying and why. She naturally asked after you.' He shrugged. 'It's the type of person she is.'

Vicky was a little overawed at this information but decided to receive it as nonchalantly as he gave it.

'They'd like to come and see the beautiful McLoughlin Vale next weekend.'

'How long would they stay?'

'Just for the day. Although Kath would like to stay the night, she prefers her own bed—especially being pregnant.'

'I hope the cramping has stopped.'

'It has. She'll be thirty weeks next weekend—and counting! Kath keeps telling me she's on the downhill straight—only ten weeks to go.'

'That's if she's not overdue.' Vicky pointed out. 'Generally, with first pregnancies the baby is late.'

'It had better not be in this case. Kathryn can't stand waiting around. She's so impatient. I'll bet that from thirty-seven weeks onwards she'll be doing everything in her power to bring the baby on.' Steven laughed and Vicky joined in.

Once they'd finished dinner and tidied the kitchen, Vicky suggested they go for a walk, instead of watching television. 'It's a lovely night.'

'How can you say that?' Steven countered. 'There are gathering thunderclouds and the air is thick with the promise of rain.'

'That's what I mean. The calm before the storm.' Vicky walked to the back door and waited for Steven to join her. 'You can smell the promise of rain.'

'It's humid enough not to warrant a coat.' Steven closed the door behind them. 'If we get wet we get wet.'

'Precisely.' Vicky felt a bubble of happiness threaten to spill over into girlish giggles. The urge increased when Steven clasped his hand warmly with hers and tugged her down the back steps.

They walked down past the chicken coop and on towards the boundary between Vicky's land and Leesha's.

'How are things progressing with the cottage?' Vicky asked. Up until now she'd forgotten all about the renovations.

'Should be about another seven to ten days. I spoke to David—the managing director of Sharlock—yesterday when I was in the city,' he explained. 'Would you like to have a look and see how things are progressing?'

'No. Thank you,' she added as an afterthought. 'Going

over there, it reminds me of all I've lost. I saw surveyors on Jerome's land the other day so I guess it won't be long until he sells.'

'It really upsets you, doesn't it?' Steven stopped walking and wrapped his arms about her waist.

'It does but I'm slowly coming to terms with it. I feel as though I'm losing a member of my family, the way previous generations have cultivated and cared for this land.' Taking a deep breath, Vicky put a smile on her face. 'But I really don't want to talk about it now. At the moment I'm happy and content with life.'

'Which is how it should be.' Steven returned her smile, before slowly lowering his head to claim her lips.

The kiss was soft and delicious, sending a warm feeling to the pit of Vicky's stomach. This was the man she loved and he was kissing her so very tenderly. If only he would give her some indication of his true feelings. Perhaps…perhaps then she might allow herself to dream of a future *with* him.

When he drew away from the kiss, Steven held her close. Listening to his heart beating beneath his shirt, Vicky knew she'd come home and marvelled at how complete she felt. Now all she had to do was convince Steven he felt the same.

'Steven…' She lifted her head to look into his eyes. 'I…need to tell you—'

'Don't,' he whispered, pressing a brief kiss to her lips. He must have read the expression on her face—desire mixed with confusion and love. What a combination, she thought as she rested her head against his chest again.

'One step at a time, remember?'

The sky lit up behind them with a display of lightning and they turned to watch.

'Amazing, isn't it?' Steven's arms still held her firmly.

'Majestic,' Vicky agreed, as the sky lit up time and time again.

'The rain will be here soon. We'd better start heading back.'

Both remained silent as they walked back towards the house, hand in hand, stopping now and then to watch more of mother nature's pyrotechnic displays. They had just reached the back steps when the first large droplets of water began to pelt down, quickly turning the ground into a quagmire.

'Good timing.' Steven said as they went inside. They spent the rest of the evening discussing different topics of medicine, arguing good-naturedly over their sometimes different opinions.

It set the pattern for the week to come where whoever arrived home first would start dinner. Then they'd spend their evenings deep in discussions about a variety of topics. Or taking long walks. Sometimes they'd watch a movie but at the end of every wonderful evening Steven would kiss her sweetly goodnight and walk away.

Vicky almost began to doubt her womanly powers. Wasn't he attracted to her any more? Had she come on too strong? Had her love been reflected so often in her eyes it scared him away? When she'd told him she didn't want an affair, she hadn't meant him to stop making *all* advances towards her. Each night, Vicky would accept his kisses, before going to bed confused but ready for sleep nonetheless.

The following Friday, as they were sharing a leisurely brunch, the phone rang. Vicky was closest and reached for the phone.

'Dr Hansen,' she said, as she swiped Steven's hand away from the half-eaten muffin on her plate.

'Vicky.' Nicole's voice was calm but held a hint of urgency. 'Is Steven with you?'

'Yes, he is,' Vicky replied, not feeling the slightest bit embarrassed any more. It was readily accepted by the townsfolk that something was going on between their GP and the new orthopaedic surgeon but whatever it was it was their business, although most of them *were* getting ready for wedding bells.

Steven looked at her, his 'doctor' façade in place.

'Nicole,' Vicky mouthed silently, and he nodded.

'Good,' Nicole said. 'Mac's just called. Susie Hartford was roller-blading and fell, breaking her right arm. Her asthma has flared up and she's not doing too well.'

'The fall must have triggered the attack,' Vicky stated. 'No doubt her mother or Mac has helped her have some Ventolin.'

'Yes, but I don't think it will be enough.'

'Right. Have some betamethasone standing by. We'll leave immediately.'

'You'll probably arrive at the same time as the ambulance, so everything will be ready and waiting,' Nicole said in her usual calm, efficient tone.

Vicky hung up as Steven rose from the table and reached for his keys.

'Details?'

Vicky quickly went into her room to pull her shoes on and grabbed her bag.

'Susie Hartford,' she replied as they shut the door behind them and climbed into Steven's Range Rover. 'Fifteen-year-old girl with bad asthma. I saw her nearly two weeks ago in my clinic for a repeat prescription. Her chest was a bit tight then but after all…' she shrugged '…it is spring. She's broken her arm, which has—'

'Caused the asthma to flare up.' Steven finished. 'Did Nicole give a report of the break?'

'No.'

'Will we get there before them?' His tone was sharp and Vicky knew what his underlying meaning was. Why did she live so far out? That was what he was thinking. She held on to her temper, but only just, as he drove over the dirt roads which were now familiar to him.

'Either that or at the same time. Everything will be fine,' Vicky said in a clipped tone.

Neither of them spoke again but the atmosphere around them was thick with tension.

They arrived at the hospital with a whole three minutes to spare before the ambulance arrived. During that time Vicky checked the things she would need while Steven ascertained from Nicole that the break was a clean one.

The wail of the ambulance siren stopped and within seconds Susie was in front of them, gasping for breath, with an oxygen mask over her face.

'Nebuliser with betamethasone, stat,' Vicky ordered. Susie was looking wildly around the room, her body trembling with fright. 'It's fine, Susie,' Vicky soothed. 'Everything is going to be all right.' She stroked the girl's forehead as the oxygen mask was replaced with the nebuliser. 'Breathe deeply. That's it, nice, deep breaths.'

'Pulse one hundred and five, BP, one-twenty over one hundred,' Nicole said quietly, for Vicky's ears only.

'Deep breaths,' Vicky urged again. 'You're breathing in an increased dose of a bronchodilator drug which will help open those airways,' she told Susie, whose eyes were now fixed firmly on hers. 'There's nothing to worry about, Susie. You're doing just fine. Nice and slow.'

For the next ten minutes everyone focused on relaxing Susie as much as possible. Staying calm was an effective measure when someone was having an asthma attack, and Vicky knew that Mrs Hartford's actions would have been just that. Over the years she'd seen her daughter through her fair share of attacks and was more than willing to be educated in whatever procedures were necessary.

Vicky looked up towards the doorway, where the girl's worried mother stood. Nicole had just reported Susie's pulse and blood pressure to be returning to normal, as indeed was her breathing.

Vicky motioned with a slight movement of her head for Mrs Hartford to come over. 'Here's your mum, Susie,' she said in the same calm tone. 'Isn't she doing a great job, Mrs Hartford?'

Susie's eyes flicked to her mother's and held. 'You're doing wonderfully, as always,' Mrs Hartford replied, and bent to kiss her daughter. This action relaxed Susie even more and within another ten minutes Vicky was able to decrease the corticosteroid intake.

'My arm,' Susie said, still gasping slightly with the mask over her nose and mouth.

'Does it hurt?' Vicky asked, relieved to hear Susie's attempt at speech. A barely imperceptible nod came from the teenager. 'Mr Pearce is here to take care of that,' Vicky said and, as if on cue, Steven stepped forward.

'Hi, Susie. I'm Steven Pearce.' His eyes met the girl's and she gave him a shy smile. 'Now that you're feeling better, I'll give you some analgesics to take away the pain in your arm. From what I can see, it's a nice, clean break but I'll need to get some X-rays of it first. Once that's done we'll put a plaster cast on.'

Vicky stepped to one side and watched Steven reassure their patient. His caring, tender attitude endeared him to her even more and she felt her heart constrict with love for him.

'Vicky?' Nicole spoke quietly, a hint of concern in her voice.

'Sorry. What did you say?'

Nicole frowned. 'Are you all right?'

'Yes. Why? Of course I am. Why? Don't I look all right?' Vicky blurted in a whisper.

The experienced nursing sister smiled. 'Forgive my intrusion. I see now that you are indeed perfectly fine.'

'What's that supposed to mean?' Vicky asked sceptically.

'You're in love with Steven,' Nicole stated quietly. 'I was wondering how long it would take you to realise it for yourself.'

'Am I that obvious?'

'Only to those who know you.'

'Great,' Vicky sighed. 'That means most of the town knows.'

Nicole laughed. 'Never mind. Steven would like you to assist with the plastering so why don't we get set up? Once Susie is back from Radiology, you'll be ready to proceed.'

Vicky focused on the room around her and saw that Susie was being wheeled out on the trolley. Steven sat down to write up the notes, before handing the file to Vicky.

'Your turn,' he said with that heart-warming smile—a smile she would never tire of seeing. 'I'll be in Radiology if you need me.'

'Sure.' She nodded and took the notes. When he'd gone, Nicole placed a comforting hand on her shoulder.

'You do have it bad, don't you?'

'I certainly do.' Vicky shook her head, still unable to decide what her next course of action should be. Should she throw herself at Steven? Should she let him dictate the pace? Should she—?

'I'm off to the plaster room. See you there,' Nicole said, interrupting Vicky's thoughts.

Turning her attention to the task at hand, Vicky proceeded to write up Susie Hartford's notes, adding her signature beneath them. She looked at Steven's handwriting and signature. Clear and legible. Surprising for a doctor. Her own writing was atrocious.

They met in the plaster room and performed the sticky task on Susie's arm. When the teenager had been wheeled to the ward, Steven wanted to check up on Fred.

'I'll come with you,' Vicky said and the two of them went to the ward.

'How's the young girl?' Fred asked the second he saw them.

'She's progressing nicely,' Vicky answered. 'Stabilised and for the moment breathing and resting quite peacefully.'

Fred relaxed back amongst his pillows. 'Good to hear. Good to hear,' he said. 'Must have given her mum a nasty shock as well as herself, I'd imagine.'

'Yes,' Vicky replied. Steven checked Fred's chart at the end of the bed and announced himself still satisfied with the observation results.

'And how's Molly coping?' Fred asked, a worried look on his face.

'Holding her own. Frank and Mavis are with her.'

'Good. I hope Daniel finds the fiend who did this and brings him to justice.'

'Unfortunately,' Steven said with a shake of his head, 'that hasn't happened yet.'

'Daniel is pursuing every lead,' Vicky added, 'but these things take time.'

'That they do,' Fred agreed. 'At least with her aunt and uncle there, it should help Molly to sleep at night.'

Molly was a constant concern at the back of Vicky's mind. Every time she'd visited the vet had appeared to be fine, but little things, such as observing the way she'd jumped when one of her dogs had barked, had made Vicky realise things were not as good as Molly insisted they were.

The community had rallied once again and Vicky knew from her daily conversations with Mary that Molly was being protected in every way she could. Mary's own progress was as stable as Vicky could hope in the circumstances. Mary and Jeff had accepted what had happened to their baby but they would never forget him.

Saturday morning dawned with a breathtaking sunrise— Vicky knew because she'd had trouble sleeping. Having

Steven so close, yet so far away, it was beginning to drive her crazy. A chaste kiss goodnight caused her fantasies to burn into overdrive and the longings were getting harder to cope with.

'Good morning.' His deep voice washed over her and she sighed in acceptance of it.

Pulling her robe tighter, she smiled at him. He was dressed in denim jeans and T-shirt, and the way they accentuated every part of his body made her tremble.

'Coffee?' she asked, and her voice squeaked on the word.

'Please.' He nodded. 'You're up early.'

Vicky cleared her throat before speaking as she poured his coffee. 'Couldn't sleep.'

'That makes two of us,' he mumbled, and ran a hand through his hair.

Vicky handed him the cup and went out of the back door to sit on the steps. Steven joined her, looking over the land. Both were silent, absorbed in their own thoughts.

She could feel the warmth of his thigh pressed up against her own and realised their dangerous position. Until she could figure out exactly what to do about her feelings she was forced to stay in no man's land. Searching her mind for a neutral topic, Vicky asked, 'What time is your sister due to arrive?'

'Around eight-thirty.' He smiled. 'Kath isn't sleeping too well.'

'That's natural in her condition.'

'Yeah, but getting her husband up and ready to leave by seven-thirty, especially when it's the only day he doesn't need to go to the hospital, won't be easy.'

'Do you think they'll be delayed?'

'No. Kath will have him ready whether he likes it or not.'

'Good. I'm looking forward to meeting them, but first things first. I'll go to the hospital and check on Susie then I have a few house calls to make. If I try to get them over and done with by the time Kathryn and Jack arrive, I should be free for the day.'

'Your patients won't still be in bed, will they?' Steven drained his coffee-cup.

'No. I usually see them first thing Saturday morning. Old Mrs Swaine has bad leg ulcers. The district nurses take care of the dressings but I like to check her once a week. My other regular call is to Mr Matthews. He's been in a wheel-chair for the past thirty years, following a terrible tractor accident. Again, the district nurses do a great job but neither of these patients can get into the clinics for checks so Saturday mornings it is.'

'The life of a country GP,' Steven quipped.

'Exactly, and sitting here talking to you isn't going to get the work done.' She stood and went inside.

Under the spray of the shower Vicky gave herself a stern lecture about Steven Pearce. When she'd towelled herself dry she became lenient once again, and after she'd finished dressing she was ready to fall into his arms, regardless of his feelings for her.

'You can't go on like this,' she told her reflection. 'Go and see your patients. Focus,' she commanded, but realised it was easier said than done.

Susie Hartford was coming along fine. Her breathing had stabilised and with her usual medications everything was working like clockwork.

'You can go home today,' Vicky said, and the teenager smiled with delight.

'Thank you, Dr Hansen,'

'I know Mr Pearce is happy with your arm, although he'll need to see you in around six to eight weeks so you can have the plaster removed, but I'm sure he discussed this with you yesterday.'

'Yes, he did,' Susie replied.

'Good.' Vicky wrote in the notes and then said, 'I'd like

to see you in one week for a review on your asthma. Other than that, take it easy the next time you decide to roller-blade.'

'I will, Dr Hansen.' Susie nodded seriously.

Fred was still sleeping when Vicky quickly went around to the men's ward so, after getting an update on his night's progress, which had been uneventful, she left the hospital to complete her house calls.

She squashed down the nervousness she felt that kept rising every time she thought about meeting Steven's sister. Some sisters had a lot of influence over their siblings and she couldn't help but wonder if this was some sort of test Steven wanted her to undergo before he made any serious commitment to her.

When Vicky returned to her house after the non-eventful house calls, there was a black XK 20 Jaguar parked in the shed. Did his whole family have Jaguars? It was a lovely car and, after taking a closer look, Vicky decided she could delay the inevitable no longer and went inside, the knots in her stomach as tight as a drum.

'Here she is,' Steven announced when she entered the kitchen.

Vicky's pasted-on smile relaxed into a real one as she was greeted warmly by Steven's sister and her husband. Kathryn was a stunning woman, with long auburn hair flowing loosely around her shoulders.

'I'm sorry we've barged into your house like this but Steven insisted it would be fine.' She put a hand to the side of her mouth and said in a stage-whisper, 'Men don't think along the same lines as women.'

'Amen to that,' her husband Jack added. 'I'm Jack Holden. Pleased to meet you, Vicky.' Jack was tall with dark hair and blue eyes that softened with love whenever he looked at his wife.

Vicky frowned for a moment and looked from Steven back to Jack. 'Jack *Holden*. The famous *neurosurgeon*?'

'Your reputation has preceeded you again, darling,' Kathryn teased.

'I'm sorry. I didn't mean to gush,' Vicky apologised quickly. 'Steven never told me your surname. I've read your publications and found them not only interesting but extremely useful as well.'

'Thank you, Vicky.' Jack beamed. 'Glad my experience was beneficial to you.'

'Oh, she's good,' Kathryn said to Steven. 'She's very good. You've won Jack over for life, Vicky. Tell him you think he's a marvellous neurosurgeon and it goes straight to his head.' She laughed at her own joke. 'If I weren't happily married to him, I'd be jealous.'

Jack placed a protective arm around his wife. 'You know I only have eyes for you, but unfortunately the information and techniques I write about I need to share with everyone else.'

'Are we going to start this tour or not?' Steven asked.

'We're going.' Kathryn stood. 'As soon as Vicky tells me where to find her bathroom, we'll be almost ready to leave.' She gave her stomach a fond caress, before following Vicky's directions.

They started the tour at one of the less popular wineries— a favourite of Vicky's—and she introduced them to the owners. Everywhere they went people greeted Vicky's guests as old friends, and she could tell it pleased not only Jack and Kathryn but Steven as well.

'This is a great introduction for me also,' he commented as they left the fourth winery and headed to Faith's café for lunch. 'Thanks, Vicky.'

Over lunch, Vicky couldn't keep quiet anymore. One question had been plaguing her all morning. Apart from

Steven and herself tasting one wine each, no one had drunk a single drop.

Jack had bought several wines on her recommendation and Kathryn a few knick-knacks, but other than that—nothing.

'I can't drink, for obvious reasons,' Kathryn answered her question, 'and Jack gave up drinking many, many years ago.'

'Then why go to the wineries?' Vicky asked, still puzzled.

'I find it interesting to visit the actual wine cellars. The ambience and atmosphere of the different lifestyle intrigues me,' Kathryn told her. 'Jack won't drink any of the wines we've bought today but they're nice to have as gifts for some of our close friends, and with your personal recommendation we know they'll be excellent.'

'Thank you.' Vicky smiled at the compliment.

'And Steven,' Kathryn continued. 'Steven doesn't drink much because of a particular vascular registrar,' his sister teased.

'I know,' Vicky replied. 'He told me.'

'Really?' Kathryn's eyebrows rose in astonishment. 'And has he told you about all his other girlfriends over the years? Really, Steven, I didn't think it was your policy to kiss and tell.'

'Now, now, Katie, darling,' Jack chimed in. 'You're embarrassing him.'

'That's what big sisters are for.' She laughed. 'Besides, he knows I'm only teasing.' She snapped her fingers, as though just remembering something. 'Now where did I put those baby photos?'

'That's enough,' Steven said with mock seriousness. 'I'm sure Vicky's heard all she cares to hear.'

'Speak for yourself.' Vicky laughed. 'Where can I get my hands on those photos?'

'I'll get my mother to post some to you,' Kathryn whispered when Steven shot her another penetrating look.

After visiting some more wineries, having a tour of the hospital and a small bite for dinner, Kathryn and Jack said their goodbyes.

'Thank you for showing us around today,' Kathryn said to Vicky. 'It's been fun.' Jack helped his pregnant wife into the car. 'Take care of my little brother,' she instructed with a mischievous grin.

'I think he can manage that all by himself,' Vicky replied, and Kathryn shook her head.

'That's not what I meant. Don't be a stranger next time you're in the city, Vicky.'

As they waved goodbye, Steven placed his arm around Vicky's shoulders and pulled her to him for a kiss.

'What was that for?' she asked when they drew apart.

'I could lie and say it was a thank-you kiss for playing hostess today and making my sister happy, but the truth is...I just needed to kiss you again.'

CHAPTER TEN

THE following Wednesday evening, after Vicky had completed a very full clinic, she thankfully drove through the gates of her property, wondering whether Steven would be back from his operating list at Victor Harbour.

Ever since Steven's sister had left on Saturday evening, Vicky felt as though she'd been walking on air. Although their relationship still remained platonic, Steven had opened up to Vicky, sharing things he'd never told anyone before.

He'd talked openly about his family, the effect his eldest sister's death had had on them. He told Vicky how he'd decided to become a doctor, some of the challenges he'd faced during his internship and some of the practical jokes he'd played on colleagues.

And somehow...somehow Steven had managed to get Vicky to tell him about her family. About her parents' death, the estranged relationship between Leesha, Jerome and herself. How the community was her true family.

Eagerly Vicky continued along the dirt driveway, admiring the pinks and oranges of the sunset. They'd been experiencing a mix in weather—as was usual at this time of year in South Australia. One day it was sunny and bright and the next brought thunderstorms with lightning.

Seeing a movement from the corner of her eye, Vicky turned her head and looked out over her brother's land. Stamping her foot on the brake in anger, she saw Nigel Fairweather's gun-metal grey Ferrari parked near the boundary.

Easing her car off the dirt track, she drove closer, fury

bubbling within her. When she drew closer she stopped the car and stalked over to confront him.

'What do you want?' she asked directly. 'Do you have permission to be on my brother's land?'

'You'd prefer it if I didn't, wouldn't you?' he said. 'You'd just *love* calling up that excuse for a police officer and having me physically removed for trespassing. Well, you can forget it. Yes, I have permission from your brother to be here. We spoke only a few hours ago. Apparently, he hasn't been keeping you up to date with his affairs, but it looks as though he's finally decided to sell.'

Vicky stamped her foot in agitation but Nigel didn't laugh. He seemed to reciprocate her feelings and for a moment she was decidedly puzzled. Not wanting to say anything that would allow him to score more points, she dug her hands into her trouser pockets and waited for him to continue.

'I asked for another opportunity to look the property over and he agreed, but I doubt if I'll be able to equal or offer higher than Sharlock. They've managed to impress your brother by offering a further ten thousand over my initial price.' Nigel looked down at his expensive Italian shoes.

'Why are you telling me this?' Vicky asked cautiously. 'If I ever decide to sell, any offer you make me will obviously be improved by Sharlock Winery—especially when you consider that my land is between the two properties they own.'

Nigel grunted. 'You'll never sell. I've tried every ploy, every trick, that has worked with others but on you they simply slide off like Teflon.'

'Thank you.' Vicky smiled. 'I take that as a compliment.' She watched him for a few seconds, his eyes cast down to his shoes again. What was he up to? she wondered.

'Are you trying to soften me up, Nigel?' she asked, and from the guilty expression on his face she guessed she was correct. 'You want me to talk to my dear, sweet, brother on your behalf, don't you? Well, you can think again. I have no intention of speaking to Jerome about you or anyone else buying the land, and as far as me ever selling out to you—it will never happen. Never! *If* I *ever* in the future decide that I no longer want this land, which is extremely doubtful, I would not, in my wildest dreams, sell to you. You are the last person on earth I'd want getting their clutches on my family land.

'I wasn't exactly thrilled when Leesha sold but I was relieved it wasn't to you. Now you've just given me all the satisfaction I need by admitting Jerome is likely to accept Sharlock's offer over yours. Oh, I bet you'll match and even better the price, but Sharlock, by the sound of it, can still top any offer you make and you know it.' Vicky took a few angry steps away from the fence.

'You've done what you came to do, Nigel Fairweather, and I sincerely hope you had to wait a very long time for me to return so you could put your little plan of trying to get me to feel sorry for you into action. But it backfired—in a big way. Now, get off my brother's land. Permission or not, I'll have you removed for squatting if you're not gone within half an hour.'

With that, Vicky turned and walked briskly back to her car. She refused to look back, although she was certain Nigel was throwing imaginary daggers her way. He had all the tactics, all the business strategies and all the tricks of the trade down pat, but he'd failed with her and the knowledge made her feel stronger.

When she parked her car in the shed she was still fuming. She was mad at Jerome, mad at Nigel and mad at the Sharlock Wine Company. All of them were responsible for the ruin of her heritage, Jerome especially.

She slammed the back door behind her and Steven called

out from the kitchen. Dumping her bag and keys on the floor, she stormed in.

'Hi,' he said as he stirred a pot on the stove. 'Dinner's almost ready. Would you like a drin—?' He stopped as he picked up on her attitude. 'What's wrong?'

'My brother has sold.'

'I see.' Steven turned the stove off, wiped his hands and enveloped her in a hug. He waited.

'I've just had a confrontation with that…that weasel Nigel Fairweather.'

'What did he want?'

'You'll never believe it. He wanted me to talk to Jerome on his behalf—*his* behalf—to try and stop Jerome from selling to Sharlock.' Vicky broke free from Steven's embrace and began to pace the room.

'What did you say?' Steven asked calmly.

'What do you think I said? Not a chance. I would never help that lying, cheating piece of slime. I'm not too impressed about Sharlock owning both pieces of land but it's a far better prospect than that contemptible pig owning them.'

Steven was silent during her tirade and Vicky looked up at him. 'Sorry. I didn't mean for you to bear the brunt of my frustration and anger.'

Steven shook his head. 'If anyone deserves it, I do.'

'Why?'

'Sit down, Vicky. There's something I need to tell you.' Vicky frowned. 'What's wrong?'

'Just sit down, please.' He urged her over to the table and forced her to sit. 'It's been eating at me for too long and I have to confess the truth.'

'Steven, you're beginning to scare me.' A feeling of foreboding surrounded her as she gave him her complete attention.

'The Sharlock Wine Company.' He stood before her, his face unreadable. 'I'm a director and silent partner.'

The impact of his words hit Vicky with full force. Her anger, which had started to diminish, surged to life. Accompanying the anger was disbelief, disappointment and dejection.

'You used me,' she said quietly, 'You lying, cheating—' She rose to her feet. 'You're as bad as Nigel Fairweather. No.' She rounded on him. 'You're worse. At least he's up front about being slime. You—you're deceitful. What was the plan, Steven? To woo the land from me?' Vicky's decibel level began to rise as her wrath increased. 'Was I your *assignment*?' She said the last word as though it were filthy.

'Vicky, I'm sorry. It wasn't like that.' Steven tried to defend himself but it was no use. Vicky was in a full-blown rage and there was nothing he could do.

'You used me. You lied to me. You…you made me fall in love with you and just when I believed everything was rosy you drop this bombshell on me. How could you?

'No wonder you were so eager to persuade me to move closer to town. You weren't concerned for the people of this community—you just wanted my land. Just *doing your job*! And you actually had me questioning the level of care I provide here. Questioning whether you were right. Did I live too far out? Did it really matter? Yet all the time the whole thing was a ploy for your own selfish gain.

'How could I have been so blind? I even discussed this with Mary to try and get a different perspective, and do you know what she said?' Vicky gave a short laugh of derision. 'She actually suggested your motives for persuading me to move might have been because you wanted to start a life with me. Live in a house that was ours, not just mine. She helped me believe that your motives were honourable, that perhaps you were in love with me and wanted us to spend the rest of our lives together.

'Oh, how wrong she was and how naïve I was to believe it. You're incapable of feeling such lowly and human emotions. All you can see is dollar signs. I realise that if Sharlock were to own all three parcels of this land, it would make them a lot of money. Well, you can tell your colleagues that it will never happen. I said it to the weasel and I'll say it to you. I will *never* sell.'

When she was silent for a moment, Steven raised an eyebrow in question. 'Finished?'

'Yes,' she said more calmly. 'I'm finished. Completely. Finished with the likes of Nigel Fairweather, finished with the Sharlock Wine Company and definitely finished with you.'

Tears began to well in her eyes and she brushed them away impatiently. Steven took a step closer.

'Don't. Don't you dare touch me. I want nothing to do with you, Steven Pearce. Absolutely nothing. Get your things and get out of my house. I don't care where you go or what you do. Just get out of my sight, out of my house and out of my life.'

Vicky turned and ran to her bedroom, throwing herself onto her bed. The tears began to flood from her eyes as the enormity of her misery engulfed her. How could he? How could the man she loved with all her heart, soul and mind have turned out to be such a deceptive…stranger?

When the board meeting was at last over, Steven stayed where he was as everyone else left the room. He stretched his arms over his head, flexing his tired muscles. He could really use one of Vicky's massages about now. She'd understand.

His clinic and operating list had seemed to drag on for ever. Then he'd had the meetings here, at the Sharlock Wine Company, but finally the moment he'd been impatient for had arrived.

'David.' He spoke to the managing director who was making a final notation, before gathering up his notes. 'We need to talk.'

'Problem?' his friend asked.

'Big one.' Steven stood and began to pace the length of the room. David leaned back in his chair and waited.

'It has to do with...Victoria Hansen.' Even when Steven spoke her name his voice held a hint of longing.

'I thought as much,' David replied, a grin spreading across his face. 'I told you to be careful.'

'What's that supposed to mean?' Steven demanded tersely.

'Nothing.' David held up his hands in defence. 'Let me guess. She won't sell.'

'No, and I refuse to pressure her any more. Vicky sees the land as her family heritage. It's a part of her, especially the house. She's very different from her siblings and the fact that they've sold has strengthened her determination *not* to sell.'

'Fine. If you're positive she doesn't want to sell then we won't pressure her.' David shrugged. 'We have the land on either side, which is ample to achieve our goals. It was worth a shot and I know you would have done your best.' David raised his eyebrows and asked with mock innocence, 'Didn't you have some tactics up your sleeve?'

Steven raked a hand through his hair in frustration. 'Tactics! Huh! Who was I trying to kid? On any other woman they might have worked, but on Vicky...' He shook his head. 'On Vicky they just made matters worse. She's far too strong-willed to be dictated to—by anyone. No. Vicky Hansen isn't like other women.'

'Not vulnerable like that redhead in Naracoorte?'

'Nowhere near it. Vicky is stubborn. Forthright. Gets under your skin.' He clenched his fists, then took a deep breath and forced himself to relax. 'She's also caring, sensitive, giving…' Steven paused as he recalled the way she'd looked after he'd kissed her. 'Passionate.' The word was said with tenderness as he remembered the wild anticipation in her dark eyes when he'd held her close. Her hair all messed up from his hands. Her lips slightly swollen and her breathing heavy as she'd waited expectantly for his next onslaught. She was driving him insane!

'Ding!' David said, as though imitating a timer. 'This goose is cooked.'

Steven snapped his attention back to David. 'Meaning?'

'You're in love, mate.'

'I'm *what*?' Steven asked incredulously.

'In love with Victoria Hansen. You have fallen big time and the sooner you admit it, the happier you'll be.' David's smile increased. 'Happens to the best of us, buddy,' he said as he twirled his wedding ring.

Steven sat down in the chair with a thud. 'Love?'

'Yes. Do you know how Vicky feels?'

'I know *perfectly* how she feels. Once I told her I was a director here she didn't want anything to do with me. She feels I lied to her, betrayed her—and she's right. I did. I doubt she'll ever forgive me.'

'Nah! Women are like that when they're angry.' David brushed away his words. 'How did she feel *before* you told her?'

'Fantastic.' Steven grinned sheepishly at his friend. 'She's one incredible woman, Dave.'

'Then what are you going to do about it?'

'You're right.' Steven picked up his briefcase. 'If you'll excuse me, I have some things to organise. Thanks.'

'Any time. Just as long as I'm best man at the wedding,' David directed, then shook Steven's proffered hand.

'Vicky.' Nicole's voice came urgently over the line as Vicky held the receiver to her ear, trying in vain to drag herself from sleep. 'It's Molly. Her place has been attacked again by the drug-user—only this time it's worse.'

Nicole's words hit like a bucket of ice water and Vicky was instantly alert. 'What's happened?' She clambered out of bed and cradled the phone between her ear and shoulder as she frantically dressed. Checking the clock, she saw it read half past five.

'In a nutshell, the guy came back but this time he had a shotgun.'

'What!' Vicky exploded.

'Molly's fine—physically. But it's Frank, Vicky. He shot Frank in the leg.'

'Where are they?' she asked.

'Still out at Molly's place. Daniel's just phoned here. Do you know when Steven is due back from Adelaide?'

'Some time this morning. He'd be on his way by now so it shouldn't be too much longer.'

'I'll keep trying his mobile. He's obviously temporarily out of range. Mac's on his way to Molly's place and will meet you there. Molly told Daniel the guy was so high when he arrived that he wouldn't have known what he was doing. He held the gun to Molly's head until she produced some ketamine. Then he quickly injected it, before leaving. That was when Frank tried to capture him and was shot. Be very careful when you go out there because at this stage Daniel has no idea where he is.'

'Right. I'll see you at the hospital.' Vicky quickly rang off. Throwing the phone down on to the bed, she tucked in her shirt and pulled on her shoes. Next she collected her medical bag, which was always packed for emergencies, and her keys and went to the door.

She opened it, looked outside—then closed it promptly. It was teeming down with rain so she hauled on her large, warm raincoat and pushed her feet into gumboots. Picking up the bag and keys again, she headed for the car.

Switching on the headlights, Vicky drove carefully to Molly's. The rain had turned the dirt roads to slick mud so she engaged the four-wheel-drive converter and proceeded on her way.

The only sound was the windscreen wipers as they swished frantically over the windshield. Vicky kept a close eye out for the junkie, as Nicole had warned her. High on ketamine, the man wouldn't have had a clue what was happening around him.

Considering Nicole had said he'd already been high when he'd arrived at Molly's, the chances of him falling into a K-hole were great. If Daniel and his search party couldn't find him, death could well be a possibility for the junkie.

Vicky slowed to turn into Molly's drive then concentrated on negotiating the twists and turns over small hills that would eventually lead to the vet's house. Coming over the last rise, Vicky stopped her car and reached for her bag.

Turning to open the door, she saw another car—a red Range Rover—pull up beside her. Steven! He was here. Her heart leapt with the knowledge before she remembered the emergency.

Tugging the hood over her head, Vicky climbed from the car, bag in hand.

'Glad you could make it,' she said to Steven as they hurried to the verandah.

'So am I.'

The faint sounds of the ambulance siren could be heard. 'Glad to see Mac could come to the party,' Steven said without humour. 'Let's assess the damage.'

Frank was in a back room of the house which doubled as Molly's supply room. He was lying on a bed of blankets and pillows which had been shoved underneath him. Thankfully, no one had been silly enough to move him.

Steven went quickly to attend Frank while Vicky was sent to Molly's bedroom. Molly was sitting in the middle of her bed, a blanket around her shoulders. As she rocked back and forth, silent tears streamed down her face.

'Molly.' Vicky hugged the other woman. She held her for a while, raising a hand to her forehead and noticing the cold clamminess of her skin. Her pulse rate was high but not excessively so, considering the circumstances.

'I thought I was going to die,' she sobbed. 'Then when he shot Uncle Frank...' Fresh tears burst forth and Vicky held her friend as vicious sobs racked her body. Hearing a sound, she looked up to see Mac in the doorway.

'Anything you'll be needing, lass?' he asked softly.

'Diazepam, if you have it, please, and a glass of water.'

Mac disappeared but returned quickly, giving Vicky the water and tablets.

'Molly,' Vicky said softly, 'I'd like you to swallow these. It's just some Valium to help settle your nerves and allow your body time to rest and recover.'

Molly willingly took them, lacking the strength to argue. 'We'll be transferring you to the hospital later but, for now, sleep.' Vicky held her for a few more minutes, before helping her to lie down under the covers.

As she was coming out of Molly's room she bumped into Faith. 'Thank goodness you're here.' Vicky knew, as usual, that the people of this community would think nothing of being disturbed at this hour when they were needed.

'Are you staying, Faith?'

'Yes. Mavis will go with Frank to the hospital so I thought someone should be here with Molly.'

'Good. I've just given her some Valium. She shouldn't wake up for at least another four to six hours but by then I hope to have her at the hospital where she can be monitored more closely.'

'Fine,' Faith replied. 'I'll pack a bag for her so she'll be ready to leave when you give the word. Steven was asking for you a moment ago so get going, girl.'

Vicky found Steven and Mac lifting Frank's stretcher into the ambulance. Mavis was already sitting up front, waiting impatiently.

'Ready to go?' he asked Vicky. 'I'll need you in Theatre with me.'

'I'm ready.' She watched as he climbed in beside his patient. 'I'll follow you.' Her words caused him to raise his eyebrows, a twinkle in his eyes as she realised what she'd said.

'I mean…I'll follow the ambulance.'

He smiled, warming her body right down to the tips of her toes. 'Drive safely,' he instructed as she closed the rear doors of the ambulance.

The rain added an extra five minutes to their journey, but when they arrived at the hospital everything and everyone was organised. X-rays were taken of Frank's femur and studied while Emma performed her pre-operative anaesthetic check. Frank kept slipping in and out of consciousness because of the pethidine Steven had administered on site but was aware of what was happening.

'It's clear. It's clean,' Steven announced, after thoroughly reviewing the X-rays. 'Let's do it. Anaesthetise when you're ready, Emma.'

That done, Steven removed the bandage he'd previously applied and began preparing Frank's leg for the removal of the bullet. After arranging the drapes where necessary and debriding the wound, he told Vicky and the rest of the staff what his procedure would be.

'The incision will be here,' he said, pointing along the femur. 'Vicky will hold retractors and suction. There's quite a bit of blood loss, which probably means an artery has been nicked. Once I've clamped that, we can begin inspecting the muscle, nerve and other tissue damage, before hunting out that offending bullet.'

He looked around the room, meeting everyone's eyes

over the tops of their masks. When he glanced at Vicky she gave him a little nod, indicating she was ready. Without further instructions he made the incision.

Vicky held the retractors so he could see clearly into the wound, and he asked for a clamp. It was firmly placed into his hand and he secured the affected artery.

'There it is.' He asked for the theatre light to be slightly adjusted to allow him a better view. 'Nice and shiny but, oh, so deadly.' It was a good five minutes before he was able to get a decent grip on it but then he proudly lifted it out and they all listened to it clatter into the waiting kidney dish.

'One bullet successfully removed,' he announced, and received a small cheer for his efforts. 'Time to get Frank ready for a complete recovery.'

When he was satisfied, Steven unclamped the artery and sutured it, before closing the wound in layers with soluble sutures. The leg was bandaged and Emma was given the signal to reverse the anaesthetic.

Once they were finished, Vicky quickly degowned, doing her best to ignore Steven. He might be a brilliant and handsome surgeon who had captured her heart but she didn't have to like him. Especially after the way he'd betrayed her. She headed for the door.

'Vicky.' Steven placed a hand on her shoulder and turned her to face him. 'We need to talk.'

'No, we don't,' she said forcefully. 'I don't have anything to say to you.'

'Then just listen,' he implored.

Vicky tried to control her feelings. The way her heart hammered against her chest from his slightest touch. The way those darned butterflies churned in her stomach when he looked at her with those dangerously sensuous blue eyes. The way her knees refused to hold her up when she was in his presence.

She strengthened herself. 'No. I need to check on Molly—she should be here by now.' Vicky forced herself to meet Steven's gaze. 'Goodbye, Steven.'

Then she stepped away from him, turned her back and walked down the corridor, her heart breaking with every step she took.

'Has she woken at all?' Vicky asked Nicole quietly as they walked over to Molly's bed.

'She was drowsy when being transferred but, apart from that, Faith said she slept. Her breathing has been calm and controlled and on arrival her pulse was normal.'

'Good.' Vicky stood for a few minutes, watching the rise and fall of Molly's body beneath the crisp, hospital blankets. 'Don't disturb her.' They walked back to the nursing station where Vicky wrote up her treatment. 'I'll prescribe another intake of Valium in case she needs it but hopefully she won't. The more relaxed she is, the better she'll be able to deal with the mental and emotional stress ahead of her.'

'Contact Dr Rolton, the psychiatrist, as soon as possible and ask if she's available for a consult. The sooner, the better. This afternoon if she can manage it. She'll be able to help Molly through this.

'I'd rather Molly wasn't moved from the hospital or the district at the moment as I feel it would compound the problem even further, so if Dr Rolton could come here I would appreciate it. If you need me to speak with her let me know but, considering you've dealt with her before, I doubt my intervention would be necessary.'

'Yes, Doctor. If you'll dictate a referral letter, that will keep all the red-tape people happy.'

'Certainly. I'll do it now so it's out of the way.' She quickly checked her watch. 'Half an hour before my clinic starts. What a way to spend a morning.' Vicky yawned and her stomach grumbled.

'Great. That's one more thing to do before my clinic.' She sighed, feeling numb.

Knowing Steven was here in the hospital, so near yet so far, it was beginning to drive her crazy. She couldn't keep fighting the love she felt for him but it was too soon for her to analyse her feelings.

After dictating the letter for Nicole, she left the hospital, grabbed a sandwich from Faith's coffee-shop and ate it before her clinic started.

As the day wore on, so did Vicky's nerves. When the last patient finally left her room exhaustion began to set in. Everyone had wanted to discuss and receive updates on this morning's events.

She'd heard that Daniel's search party was still looking for the junkie, and Vicky knew the longer it was before the man was found, the greater the danger to his life. At the moment she didn't hold a lot of hope of Daniel finding him alive.

There was a brief knock at her door, and before she could mask her weariness Steven entered her consulting room. Vicky tried to rally the energy to ward him off but there was none to be found. She watched him cross to her desk and sit down opposite her.

'Thought you might like an update.'

'Why should you be different from anyone else I've seen this afternoon?' Vicky shrugged. 'Go ahead.'

'Frank's leg will be fine. He'll make a full recovery in time. Unfortunately, this wound will assist in the further degeneration of his hip, advancing his need for a total hip replacement.'

Vicky nodded.

Steven continued. 'I'm sure Nicole's phoned Molly's status through to you.'

'She has. Thankfully, Dr Rolton, a psychiatrist from Adelaide, has agreed to come down first thing in the morning to see Molly. For the moment, though, and under the circumstances, it appears Molly is holding her own.'

'I stopped by to see her before I came. She was sitting up, eating. Not much, I grant you, but nevertheless eating.'

'Good. Any word on the junkie?'

'Not yet but I'm sure Daniel will—' His words were cut off as Vicky's phone shrilled to life.

'Dr Hansen,' she said automatically into the receiver, unable to disguise the tiredness in her voice. She murmured a few times, before saying, 'I thought so. Thank you for letting me know.' Another pause. 'He's here. Yes, I will.'

She replaced the phone.

'Daniel?' Steven guessed.

'Yes. The junkie is dead. They found him just past the Anderson farm on the town road—face down in the mud.'

They stared at each other for a moment, the sobering news changing the atmosphere in the room. Life is too short. We're all mortal. Live for today!

'Vicky,' Steven said softly, 'we need to talk.'

'I know,' she agreed, 'but not now. I'm exhausted.'

Steven suggested they return to Vicky's place. The rain seemed to be getting worse so Vicky drove very carefully towards her home, Steven following in the Range Rover.

She was too exhausted to light a fire so they could get warm from the central gas heating, snuggle up and watch a movie. Vicky could already feel herself beginning to unwind as she imagined Steven's arms, holding her tightly to him.

She hadn't forgotten his lies and deception but her anger was rapidly diminishing. She loved him. She would listen to his explanations and she would forgive him—anything to have the heaviness removed from her heart.

As she turned her car into the driveway a flash of lightning illuminated the sky. Then another, and another. It was an awesome spectacle.

A bright fork of lightning slammed into her house—then

another. Vicky's eyes widened in horror and she sped up, unable to believe what was happening. Her heart hammered into her throat and she could hear it resounding in her ears. No. Not the house!

When she drove around to the back she could see smoke coming out of the roof above the kitchen. Braking hard, she clambered from the car and rushed blindly up the back steps. Steven was only moments behind her.

Vicky burst into the kitchen and stood still. For a split second everything seemed normal but when she looked at the ceiling she could see the paint beginning to blister.

'*No!*' The word was wrenched from her lungs as she wildly began opening cupboards and tossing things out. A plate chipped, a cup smashed, but Vicky was oblivious to everything. She saw Steven out of the corner of her eye, standing still. Why didn't he help her? Why didn't he do something?

'Daniel. Fire at Vicky's house,' he said quickly into the mouthpiece of his mobile phone, before disconnecting the call and walking up the hallway. Vicky gathered up what she could and quickly dumped it outside.

When she re-entered the house, Steven was walking towards her, shaking his head, his face grim.

'It's in the ceiling, Vicky. There's nothing we can do.'

'We have to fight it,' Vicky urged as she sped outside to find the garden hose. The wind lashed the rain into her as she switched the tap on with numb, wet fingers.

'We can't fight it,' Steven yelled, trying to make her hear him through the howling wind as he switching off the tap.

'*My home.* My home is on fire.' She went to switch the tap back on but Steven took both of her hands in his.

'Listen to me,' he ordered. Steven clamped a hand firmly on her shoulder and forced her to look at him. 'It's *too late*! The hose will accomplish nothing, Vicky. It's raining far more water than that little hose could ever pump out and the rain isn't having *any* effect.'

'But my home…' Vicky shrugged away from him and raced to the back steps.

'We only have about ten minutes before it's completely engulfed. Let's get out what we can.'

'Yes,' she agreed, nodding fervently before they went back inside. Vicky raced to her room and began collecting whatever she could get her hands on. Clothes, books, photographs. She ran to the back door and deposited them over near her car, the rain drenching everything in a matter of seconds. She discarded her raincoat as it was too cumbersome for the task she needed to do.

The thought about not being able to save her beloved home, the place which held so much of her family history, the home she'd been raised in, the rooms which held the memories of her parents and grandparents—these thoughts she pushed aside in her efforts to rescue what she could.

Steven raced through the house, collecting what he could. Unable to believe that it was happening. How could this happen to Vicky when he *knew* how much the house meant to her? All of the memories it held, the ones she cherished so much she was unwilling to part from them for any amount of money. It was all slipping away from her in a matter of minutes.

Steven piled books, videos and photographs into his arms and raced back out to the dump site. Anything to help salvage something of Vicky's heritage. Re-entering the lounge room, Steven glanced at the ceiling, his eyes stinging from the smoke. The beams were well and truly on fire now, and in a few more minutes it would collapse on them. He ripped his shirt and tied it around his mouth, urging Vicky to do the same, in the attempt to stop them inhaling so much smoke.

He crossed to the china cabinet and slid the door open.

The wood was hot and he knew his fingers would blister from the contact. Taking off his ripped and charcoal-stained shirt, Steven gently lifted Vicky's parents' precious wedding china from the cabinet, using his handkerchiefs to pad his hands. The plates had heated up as they would have done in an oven.

Vicky burst into the room, her eyes frantically searching him out, and then focused on what he was doing. She glanced quickly at the ceiling and then back to where Steven worked methodically as he collected the china.

'Leave it,' she called, but he shook his head. Perhaps, Vicky realised in that fleeting moment, Steven did understand what this place meant to her—and it was all too late. There wasn't much of a place left.

She crossed to his side.

'Here. Take this load out. I'll get the rest.'

'Leave it,' she reiterated.

'Go!' he ordered.

Vicky lifted the twelve-piece setting of dinner plates, entrée plates and bowls, and quickly carried them through the house and to safety outside. Steven had made sure every door was closed to contain the fire for as long as possible, but the heat was becoming unbearable and the smoke stung overwhelmingly at her eyes.

Vicky heard an ear-splitting crack moments after she'd placed the china on the ground.

'Steven,' she called, but the wind carried her voice away into the storm. *'Steven!'* Her call became more frantic as she stumbled back up the steps, her legs like lead as she rushed towards the lounge room.

'Steven.' She rounded the door to the lounge room and quickly raised a hand to cover her eyes. The fire had spread down the walls, setting the curtains ablaze with staggering ferocity.

Steven was balancing the last of the china in his opened

handkerchiefs and arranging it in his arms. The beams in the ceiling had begun to crack and the first fiery embers were now falling and burning themselves into her rug.

'Steven!' Vicky saw the beam begin to fall and heard another crack just as Steven made it over to the doorway.

'Let's get out of here,' he yelled as they rushed through the burning inferno which had been Vicky's family home.

Steven allowed Vicky to unload his arms before he collapsed on the ground, his legs unable to support him any more.

Vicky crossed to his side and looked at him. His body and face were covered with a sheen of sweat and soot. She collapsed beside him, drawing him closer and placing her arm around his back. He winced and the doctor in her came to the fore.

'Let me see your back,' she ordered.

'It's nothing.'

Vicky turned him around and winced. 'Steven!' His back had been burned, and there was an angry red slash across it.

'It probably looks worse than it is,' he offered.

'Come and sit in the car where it's dry.' Steven did as she asked. Collecting some antiseptic and vitamin E cream from her medical bag in the back of the car, she returned to take a closer look at his back.

'I don't know why you insisted on getting the china. You could have been killed,' Vicky said forcefully, ignoring the lump in her throat. She began cleaning the wound. 'You're right. It looks a lot worse than it is.' A lump formed in her throat as the realisation of the situation hit her. Steven had just escaped a brush with death and it made her tremble with fear. Fear of losing him.

She brushed away a tear but another one quickly formed. 'You may have a few small blisters but that'll be all.' She sniffed, unable to control her emotions any longer.

Steven turned to face her and instantly gathered her close.

'Vicky. I'm sorry about your house. I *know* how much it meant to you.'

Vicky began to sob but it wasn't for the house. She had *nearly* lost the man she loved! The house, for all its heritage and memories, *was* just a pile of nails and wood. It could be replaced with another home which would continue her family's heritage and create new memories.

Steven, however, could not. If he had been seriously injured…if that beam had fallen on him…he might have died. Vicky snuggled closer and pressed her ear to Steven's chest. She could hear his heart beating, sure and strong. He *was* alive and she loved him with all her heart. In the light of her present circumstances Steven's deception seemed insignificant.

Vicky eased away from him and blew her nose and wiped her eyes. He meant the world to her and she had to tell him.

'Steven.' Her voice broke as she looked up into his loving face.

The wail of a siren interrupted them as the fire crews arrived. Climbing from the car, Vicky and Steven watched as the volunteers diligently fought what was left of the fire. People came up, offering their condolences and promising to take care of anything she required.

The events blurred in Vicky's mind, and once the fire was out and the crews had gone she stood there and looked sadly at the charcoal mess that had once been her family home. A warm blanket had been placed around her shivering, wet body, but it did nothing to soothe the numbness she felt inside.

'Come on.' Steven urged her over to his car. 'Let's go to the cottage and get dry.'

'The cottage?' Vicky's mind was numb and she let Steven bundle her into the passenger seat and drive her away from the wreckage. The things they'd managed to save were in the back of his car, where he'd carefully arranged them.

At the end of the short drive Steven carried her from the car into the cottage. It had changed a bit since Vicky had last seen it. The plumbing was complete and the walls had been newly painted. The furnishings were sparse but contained the essentials.

'A nice hot shower and then into bed. I'll make you some tea and toast, then I want you to sleep.' When Vicky opened her mouth to protest he said, 'Doctor's orders.'

She dredged up the strength to shower and wrapped herself in a big fluffy towel. She found one of Steven's T-shirts waiting for her on the bed as he took his turn under the spray of water.

Climbing between the sheets, she towel-dried her hair and snuggled down in the warmth of the covers. There was an open fireplace in the cottage, lending an atmosphere of ambience, but tonight Vicky was pleased Steven hadn't lit it. The last thing she wanted was more fire around her.

Instead, he'd plugged in a large oil heater which was beginning to warm the place nicely. Listening to the rain outside, Vicky allowed her heavy eyelids to slowly close before she drifted off into a deep sleep.

'Some time within the next half hour.'

Vicky was dragged from sleep at the sound of Steven's voice, speaking softly to someone.

'Looks as though she's waking now. I'd better go.'

Vicky opened her eyes and looked around the room. Where was she?

'Oh, no.' She sat bolt upright in bed as the memory of the previous night's events returned in force. 'My home,' she whispered, and Steven quickly crossed to her side.

He sat down and placed an arm around her shoulders.

'I'm sorry, Vicky. I know how much that home meant to you.'

It was the same sentiment he'd expressed previously when Vicky had realised the more important facts of her situation.

'Thank you.' She ran her fingers down his face. 'The house did mean a lot to me but…' She shook her head. 'But I've realised there's more to life than a place of residence.'

Steven looked at her for a long moment, before smiling. Placing a brief kiss on her lips, he stood up and walked over to the heater. Gathering up a pair of jeans, underwear and a shirt, he handed them to Vicky.

'I managed to get these dry after you…went to sleep last night.'

Vicky looked down at the clothes and realised they were her own. Looking at Steven, she smiled in surprise. 'Thank you.' She was deeply touched by his caring gesture, and when she saw the rest of the cottage she realised that everything they'd managed to save was either stacked neatly or laid out to dry.

'The place looks a bit like a Chinese laundry so I thought we'd go out for breakfast—or should I say brunch.' He pointed to the bedside clock and Vicky gasped when she realised the time. Almost eleven o'clock.

'I've just called Faith and she's agreed you need a slap-up breakfast to help clear away your worries.'

So *that's* who he'd been talking to on the phone.

'She's expecting us soon so go and get dressed.'

Vicky did as she was told and returned a few minutes later, dragging Steven's comb through her knotted hair. That's the price she paid for sleeping with wet hair. Sleeping? She looked over to the bed she'd just vacated. That was where she had slept, but where had Steven slept?

'You were marvellous,' he teased in a sexy voice, as

though he could read her thoughts. 'You snuggled into my arms as though you belonged there.'

'I do,' she replied shyly.

'I know,' he said. 'For now, though, let's get going. I am starving.'

Steven didn't say anything on the drive to Faith's, but he did hold her hand and refused to let it go, even when he needed to change gears. Amazingly the day was bright and sunny, with all signs of yesterday's miserable weather gone. Just like that.

The coffee-shop was deserted when they went in which Vicky thought was unusual for a Saturday morning.

'Hello, dear,' Faith greeted her as she came out of the kitchen. She reached over the counter and Vicky took her hand in hers. 'I'm so sorry, Vicky. I know how much the house meant to you.'

'Thanks, Faith. I know you're all here, supporting me, and I appreciate it.'

Faith patted Vicky's hand, before letting it go. 'You must be hungry. Take a seat and I'll bring out the first course.' She disappeared back into the kitchen and Vicky turned to look at Steven, a frown on her face.

'First course?'

Steven shrugged and guided her to a table. 'Perhaps it's her way of showing she cares.'

'Probably,' Vicky agreed.

Faith soon appeared with fresh coffee and croissants. 'Eat up. Bacon and eggs are next.' She disappeared again.

'Something strange is going on.' Vicky's frown deepened. 'This place is usually swarming with people at this time of day—especially on a Saturday.'

Steven shrugged and bit into his croissant. Vicky's stomach growled in hunger so she decided to forget everything and enjoy the food—and the company.

When they had finished, Faith reappeared and cleared their plates, before bringing the next course.

'Oh, dear. The sun is getting in your eyes, Vicky,' Faith tut-tutted. 'Steven, go and pull the blinds down. I don't want anything bothering Vicky today.' And then she was gone again.

Steven stood and dutifully pulled down one of the blinds on the café windows.

Vicky's mouth dropped open and her fork clattered to the ground.

There, written in large, black letters, were the words I LOVE YOU, VICKY.

Steven crossed to the other blind, a huge smile on his face. He pulled the next blind down and she read, MARRY ME.

Steven came around and knelt by her chair, taking her left hand in his. 'Well?' he asked, and amazingly Vicky read a hint of uncertainty in his eyes.

'Are *you* asking—or is Faith?' Vicky couldn't resist teasing him.

Steven rolled his eyes and laughed. 'Who would you rather have?'

'You,' she whispered, all teasing gone. 'I love you.'

'I thought I'd ruined everything,' he said softly. 'I should have told you at the beginning about my connection with Sharlock, but I didn't. I'm sorry.'

'Shh.' Vicky placed a hand to his lips. 'I forgive you. I realised yesterday that you could have been killed in that fire. If the ceiling had collapsed on you—' She broke off, unable to complete the sentence. 'I don't care about losing the house, Steven. I wouldn't have cared about losing my parents' wedding china if you hadn't saved it. But I care— too deeply for words—about losing you.'

'Marry me, Vicky.' Steven reached into his pocket and pulled out a magnificent diamond ring.

'Yes,' she answered as he slid the ring onto her finger. 'It fits perfectly.' She smiled, echoing his earlier sentiments about how *they* fitted together.

Steven stood, bringing Vicky to her feet as well. Placing a hand on either side of her face, he bent his head to kiss her. It was a homecoming kiss full of passion and promise.

A round of applause went up and Vicky tried to push away from Steven, but found herself held tightly to him. Turning in the direction of the clapping, she saw almost half the townsfolk coming out of Faith's kitchen.

'Congratulations,' they were all saying. Mary came over and kissed Steven on the cheek, before hugging her friend.

'You were in on this, weren't you?' Vicky said accusingly.

'Of course,' Mary freely admitted. 'We all were.'

Faith poured champagne for everyone, then raised her glass in a toast. 'To Vicky and Steven,' she said.

'To Vicky and Steven,' everyone else chorused.

Vicky looked up at Steven. 'You had this whole thing planned,' she said with a shake of her head, her smile radiant.

'I told you I wasn't that easy to get rid of.' Steven kissed her again and another cheer went up.

'Thank God for that,' Vicky said softly, like a prayer. 'Thank God for that!'

MILLS & BOON®

*M*akes
any time
special

Copyright © Harlequin Enterprises Limited 1997
All rights reserved

Enjoy a romantic novel from
Mills & Boon®

Presents...   *Enchanted*™   TEMPTATION®

Historical Romance™   ▲MEDICAL
ROMANCE™

MAT1

MILLS & BOON®

MEDICAL ROMANCE™

HER FATHER'S DAUGHTER by Barbara Hart
New Author!

Dr Kate Marshall was covering a G.P. maternity leave in the Lake District. She didn't know that Dr David Firth was a partner—the man her father had thrown out of their house! She never had heard the whole story…

DIAGNOSIS DEFERRED by Rebecca Lang

Dr Laetitia Lane enjoyed emergency medicine, proud of her achievements after a troubled past. Then Dr Grant Saxby, the man who'd helped her straighten out, came back into her life, and wanted to get to know her *much* better!

THIS TIME FOREVER by Joanna Neil

Dr Mollie Sinclair coped well with the rural practice until her uncle fell ill. She didn't know her uncle had hired Dr Sam Bradley, and having just been dumped by her fiancé, Molly wasn't inclined to consider another man in a hurry!

Available from 5th May 2000

Available at most branches of WH Smith, Tesco, Martins, Borders, Easons, Volume One/James Thin and most good paperback bookshops

0004/03a

MILLS & BOON®
MEDICAL ROMANCE™

COURTING CATHIE by Helen Shelton
Bachelor Doctors

Anaesthetist Sam Wheatley longs for a child of his own, but after two years with Cathie Morris, Sam is no closer to persuading her he's a good bet as a husband. Drastic measures are called for!

TRUST ME by Meredith Webber
Book One of a trilogy

Iain and Abby McPhee were having marital problems, and Dr Sarah Gilmour wanted to help. Then television star Caroline Cordell, a local girl, was killed—was it really an accident? As the forensic pathologist, it was Sarah's job to find out, and doing so might just bring Iain and Abby together again...

Puzzles to unravel, to find love

TWICE A KISS by Carol Wood
Book Two of a duo

Nick Hansen and Erin Brooks struck sparks off each other, but Erin refused to give up her fiancé, only to be jilted at the altar. Now Nick is returning to the Dorset practice...

Available from 5th May 2000

Available at most branches of WH Smith, Tesco, Martins, Borders, Easons, Volume One/James Thin and most good paperback bookshops

0004/0

books and a surprise gift!

We would like to take this opportunity to thank you for reading this Mills & Boon® book by offering you the chance to take FOUR more specially selected titles from the Medical Romance™ series absolutely FREE! We're also making this offer to introduce you to the benefits of the Reader Service™—

★ FREE home delivery
★ FREE gifts and competitions
★ FREE monthly Newsletter
★ Exclusive Reader Service discounts
★ Books available before they're in the shops

Accepting these FREE books and gift places you under no obligation to buy, you may cancel at any time, even after receiving your free shipment. Simply complete your details below and return the entire page to the address below. *You don't even need a stamp!*

YES! Please send me 4 free Medical Romance books and a surprise gift. I understand that unless you hear from me, I will receive 6 superb new titles every month for just £2.40 each, postage and packing free. I am under no obligation to purchase any books and may cancel my subscription at any time. The free books and gift will be mine to keep in any case.

M0EA

Ms/Mrs/Miss/Mr ....Initials...................................
BLOCK CAPITALS PLEASE
Surname ....
Address ....
....
....Postcode...........................

Send this whole page to:
UK: FREEPOST CN81, Croydon, CR9 3WZ
EIRE: PO Box 4546, Kilcock, County Kildare (stamp required)

Offer valid in UK and Eire only and not available to current Reader Service subscribers to this series. We reserve the right to refuse an application and applicants must be aged 18 years or over. Only one application per household. Terms and prices subject to change without notice. Offer expires 31st October 2000. As a result of this application, you may receive further offers from Harlequin Mills & Boon and other carefully selected companies. If you would prefer not to share in this opportunity please write to The Data Manager at the address above.

Mills & Boon® is a registered trademark owned by Harlequin Mills & Boon Limited.
Medical Romance™ is being used as a trademark.

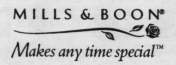

MILLS & BOON®

Makes any time special™

COMING SOON

St. Elizabeth's
Children's Hospital

A limited collection of 12 books. Where affairs of
the heart are entwined with the everyday dealings
of this warm and friendly children's hospital.

Book 1
A Winter Bride by Meredith Webber
Published 5th May

SECH/RTL/2

*Available at branches of WH Smith, Tesco,
Martins, RS McCall, Forbuoys, Borders, Easons,
Volume One/James Thin and most good paperback bookshops*